CW01390332

The Last Six Days

Emma Warhurst

Cover design by Michael Lomon.

Proofreading by Heather Gregson.

ISBN-13:
978-1507604502
ISBN-10:
1507604505

Copyright © 2014 Emma Warhurst.
All rights reserved.

Day 1

The funny thing about all of this is that I've actually always wanted to write a book. Not like this, obviously. But I always thought that one day I'd be a bestselling novelist and win all kinds of awards. I actually got a 2:1 in Comparative Literature from the University of Kent, so I'm probably brighter than people who see pictures of me in *Heat* on the red carpet at premieres might think. But I suppose that's where posing for *GQ* magazine gets you – it does overshadow a degree a bit I guess. I never wanted to do it anyway – I only agreed to it because my mum persuaded me. She was never very supportive of my literary aspirations, and I think she thought that if I was more well-known I could get a part in a reality TV series or be paid to be a spokesmodel for handbags or mascara or something , but it didn't happen. It's the kind of thing I think she wishes she'd had the opportunity to do when she was younger, but there wasn't the same celebrity culture in those days. Anyway, if *GQ* was the biggest mistake I'd made then I'd have nothing to complain about. I really would have loved to be a writer though, I just never got round to actually writing anything. But if I had done, it certainly wouldn't have been anything like this. Under the circumstances I doubt this will be anything like as good as I would have liked it to be. Not that it matters, but since it's the last thing I'm going to write...

I should have just gone to Paris. That's what I initially thought of doing, but with the Eurostar I just didn't think it was far enough away from London. Anywhere would have been better than here though. I could have gone to New York or Los Angeles to take acting lessons – plenty of people I went to school with have done that. Not that I've seen any of them in films, but I'm sure they're having a lovely time pretending to be trees or something, or learning how to do a shocked face and cry on cue. When I saw *Fame* I thought stage school looked like great fun, but in reality I'm not that confident, and I get intimidated by people who are. (In any case, I learned my lesson about confusing fiction and reality when I read all those old Enid Blyton *St Clare's* and *Malory Towers* books when I was seven, and begged my parents to send me to boarding school. To be honest I think they were already considering it anyway, so they were only too happy to agree when I suggested it. It didn't take long for me to realise that midnight feasts and nature walks were just for books, and that boarding school was actually an opportunity for girls to bully each other on a full-time basis. Persuading my parents to let me leave proved a lot more difficult, and I ended up being there for three years until I was allowed to go to a normal secondary school – private of course, but normal in the sense of being in the same school as boys and not having to share a bedroom with fifteen other people.) I could have even gone to volunteer in an orphanage somewhere. Any of these things would have been better, although in my defence I couldn't have had any idea of what I was letting myself in for here. Anyway, for some reason I was drawn to Madrid. I wanted to do something that wasn't a cliché for someone like me, and Spain seemed quite different and exciting. And at the time I was intent on showing how adventurous and independent I was. That would have worked better if I was actually either of those things, but self-awareness has never been one of my strong points. Now of course I wish I had gone anywhere else but here, or just stayed at home. But it's too late for that kind of thinking now.

Nobody can help me. Even if they could, who's going to miss me? Nobody knows me here, and my parents are on a cruise and it will probably take them weeks to even notice that I haven't emailed them. Then they'll probably think I'm just having too much fun to get in touch. But parents just know, don't they? That's what people always say. Maybe not my parents though. Anyway, how could they know? And how would they find me? Everything happened so quickly that I never even gave them my address here. No, it's impossible. I have to accept that I'm going to die. I read somewhere that Gwyneth Paltrow once thought she was dying during a barbecue, but after being rushed to hospital she apparently had a migraine and simultaneous panic attack. Lucky Gwyneth – I wish I was just being overdramatic. But no panic attack or migraine could ever be as painful as this. I never could have even imagined this level of pain before, and even now I can hardly believe that anyone can be in this much pain and still be alive, but I still am. For now at least.

It's so ridiculous that it almost seems funny now, but I came to Madrid because I felt like I needed to escape. Now I wonder what I thought I needed to escape from, but at the time I guess I was just depressed, and I was desperately trying to work out what would make me feel better, and I just thought that if I went away, everything would be different. And it's true that everything's different here, but I'm not different, I'm just myself with different scenery. So it never would have helped anyway. But people are always talking about going abroad to find themselves, and stupidly I decided that's what I needed to do: go somewhere where nobody knew who I was and find out who I really was. I don't know what I was expecting to happen really, although I could never have imagined this, even in my worst nightmares. And if I had imagined it I probably would have decided I was mentally ill and checked myself into a clinic, which in hindsight would have been a much better idea. But this isn't a nightmare – it's real, and there's nothing I can do about it.

I wasn't in a great state emotionally when I decided to come here. Ben, my boyfriend – ex-boyfriend – had broken up with me and for some reason it had hit me hard, who knows why. He'd never seemed overly keen on me even when we were together, but I guess after 18 months I'd grown attached to him. I think it was the lifestyle I liked more than him anyway – he's an actor (quite a well-known one considering how little acting he's done, even when he manages to get a part) so it meant that I got to go with him to all kinds of glamorous parties and premieres. And I suppose he liked me because my dad's rich – having no real acting talent means he's got a high profile, but not the money to back it up. He broke off our relationship with the same amount of emotion he displays on screen, and immediately got together with a lingerie model called Sophia, whose father also happens to be rich. Being replaced with a woman who was undoubtedly much more attractive than me didn't do wonders for my self-confidence, and seeing pictures of them together in the tabloids and gossip magazines every day was another reason to get out of the country for a while.

I had plenty of money in the bank, plus a regular allowance from my dad, so I couldn't think of a reason not to just go for it. And I didn't have a job keeping me in London – looking back I think having some kind of career would have really improved my self-esteem, but I haven't worked at all since I graduated, and that was over three years ago. Because my dad's restaurant chain is so successful and he can give me anything I ask for, it didn't really make sense for me to work for 40 hours a week in a low-paid job when I didn't need the money. And I never had any particular ambition anyway apart from writing, so I decided it made more sense to get as much life experience as I could for when I eventually got round to writing novels. So even though I was hurt when Ben broke up with me, in a way I felt like it might be a good opportunity to experience something completely different that might give me ideas for a book. I eventually decided that Madrid would be the best place for me, thinking that I could see the sights, learn some Spanish, and maybe meet a bullfighter or even a Spanish prince (talking of Gwyneth Paltrow, I'm pretty sure she used to date one before she married the man from Coldplay. It's probably for the best that it didn't work out – I'm not sure having a future queen called Apple would have gone down brilliantly with the Spanish royal family). Plus, unlike London, Madrid could be relied on to be hot and sunny in August, which I thought might cheer me up a bit. I booked my flights, emailed the first estate agency in Madrid that came up on Google and asked them to find me an apartment (my second mistake), and within a week I was on my way.

I arrived feeling positive about the adventures that lay ahead of me. Most of the people on the plane were holidaymakers, and the fact that I was actually going to be living in Madrid made me feel a bit smug. I had no feeling of impending doom, I just felt more excited and free than I had done for a long time. I knew the weather would be good, but the bright sunshine and the 37 degree August heat still came as a shock after the dreary London weather. It was a jump of almost 20 degrees, and stepping off the plane to walk into Barajas airport, it was almost difficult to breathe. The sun was so bright that even with sunglasses on I felt like there was someone physically pressing their thumbs into my eye sockets and I had to shield my eyes with my arm – I must have seemed like some kind of vampire who'd never seen sunshine before. But somehow the heat and the sun made everything seem exciting, and I couldn't help smiling as I headed into the airport. The officer at passport control winked at me as he handed back my passport, and I took it as a good sign, and thought to myself that I'd made the right decision in coming here. After I picked up my luggage I decided not to brave the Madrid underground on my first day here and headed to the taxi rank instead.

Not knowing any Spanish other than a few words I had picked up mainly from Shakira songs, which didn't seem particularly useful under the circumstances, I greeted the taxi driver in English and showed him the piece of paper where I had written the address of the estate agency. He asked me something in Spanish, but I had no idea what it was or how to reply so I just shrugged, and we spent the rest of the journey in silence. That was fine with me, as I could look out of the window and take in my new surroundings. As we passed seemingly endless identical blocks of flats on every street, I wondered whether I'd made a mistake in coming here (obviously I had) – laundry hanging out of windows to dry and skips on the streets with people's rubbish in them were not what I had been expecting at all. But as we approached the city centre, the apartment blocks were replaced by grand, elegant buildings, and the middle-aged women in aprons and headscarves leaning out of their windows to hang out their washing were replaced by glamorous people wandering around or sitting outside bars drinking and chatting. I couldn't help smiling again as I imagined (wrongly) that soon that would be me.

Soon we pulled up outside the estate agency, and the driver told me the price in Spanish. I had no idea what he was saying, so I handed over a 50 Euro note and hoped that it would be enough. I got some change so it must have been, and I handed over a few more coins as a tip after the driver took my suitcases out of the taxi and put them on the pavement. I wanted to ask him to wait so we could carry on to the apartment once I had picked up the keys, but I could envision a long conversation in Spanglish involving a lot of miming and me still not being able to get my message across, so I just smiled, thanked him (in English – I thought about saying *gracias* but then I thought I might say it wrong and he'd laugh at me and I'd be embarrassed, and anyway it was my first day and I thought I should ease myself in gently) and went inside.

As I entered the estate agency I was immediately greeted in Spanish by a receptionist who was a lot taller and blonder than I had been expecting – I had imagined all Spanish women would be petite with long dark hair, but obviously I hadn't properly learned my lesson about believing what I see in films, and had been assuming that all Spanish women would basically be Penélope Cruz (and hoping of course that all the men would look exactly like Javier Bardem). The woman asked me something in Spanish and I hesitated, not knowing what she was saying to me or how to answer. Realising I didn't understand, and evidently not knowing English herself, she said something else, presumably to wait a second, and hurried off, returning a few moments later with a short, balding man who appeared to be in his fifties. He asked how he could help me, speaking in such a thick Spanish accent that if I hadn't known better, I would have thought was put on deliberately to confuse me. I told him my name – Milly Somerville – and that I was here to collect the keys to my new apartment. He asked me to wait, and soon returned with a contract, which I signed without having a clue what it said, or that I was effectively signing my life away. He thanked me and handed over the keys and a card with the address of the apartment. Seemingly reading my mind, he called another taxi for me without me even having to ask, and soon I was on the way to my new home.

The apartment was in the centre of Madrid, on a street called Gran Vía, on the third floor of a huge old building that must have been a converted stately home or government building or something. The lift was broken, so by the time I got to the apartment I wasn't in the best mood, but that changed when I opened the door and looked around. The main door led straight into the living room, which had beamed ceilings, wooden floors, and cream walls with modern furniture in neutral colours, accented with colourful cushions, ornaments and blinds in burnt orange and turquoise. It wasn't what I imagined a traditional Spanish home would look like, but nevertheless it was stunning. There were no doors, but the rooms were separated by partition walls. Behind the living room on the right was the kitchen, and to the left of the living room was the bedroom with an en suite bathroom. The kitchen was modern with chrome appliances and a black and white colour scheme. There was a small balcony at the back that looked out onto a sunny internal courtyard paved with terracotta tiles, with some kind of tree in the centre, maybe an olive tree or something Mediterranean at least. The bathroom had a Moorish feel with a sunken bath and overhead shower surrounded by tea lights, and colourful patterned tiles that looked as though they could have come straight from Marrakech. In contrast to the rest of the apartment, the bedroom was quite old-fashioned and imposing, but still very attractive – all the furniture was dark wood, including a huge four poster bed that looked as though it should belong to a 17th century monarch, and beneath the window, which let some light into the room but was too high up to see out of, there was a beautiful claret-coloured leather armchair facing the bed. The light shining though a stained glass panel on the wall that separated the bedroom from the entrance hall produced colourful patterns on the wall, which made the room feel cheerful despite the darkness of the décor. The stained glass looked old, and as though it might have come straight from a church. I found the whole place breathtakingly beautiful, but somehow I felt slightly uncomfortable, although I couldn't explain why. When I was about nine, I went to a sleepover once in the school holidays at my friend Marie's house. I'd never been to a sleepover before – although I guess you could say that boarding school is like one big sleepover in a way – so I was really excited about going. I knew they lived in an old stately home, and when we pulled up to the house I thought it was like a beautiful palace from a Disney film – my mum was going through a minimalist phase, so I'd never seen anything like it before and was hugely impressed. But for some reason, once we got inside, the whole place just gave me the creeps somehow. I think it was the suit of armour in the hallway that did it – what if there was a ghost inside it, or a killer? Anyway, when we started playing hide and seek it all got too much for me, and I burst into tears. When they asked what was wrong I was too embarrassed to say I was afraid of the house, so I said I wasn't feeling very well and Marie's parents rang my dad to pick me up and take me home early. That's how I felt now, except that I couldn't ring my dad and ask him to pick me up, and anyway I was an adult now and not afraid of houses. But something just didn't feel quite right.

Oh, I forgot to mention there was also a step down from the bedroom back into the living room, which I forgot then too and tripped over. I slipped over completely and slammed the back of my head hard on the floor. It was horrible. It felt as though my brain moved in my skull, and I could taste blood in the back of my throat. I was confused to start with and didn't really know what had happened. Then, once I realised I had slipped over and hit my head, I laid still for a little while – even after I decided I was fine, I still didn't have the energy to get up. I started to cry, and managed to wipe away my tears as they rolled down the sides of my face, before they fell into my ears (I hate it when they get in your ears because you can't get them out and it's really uncomfortable, so I've always tried to avoid crying whilst lying on my back as much as possible). It was the shock more than anything that was making me cry, and the fact that there was nobody with me to care what had happened. When I got up I was still feeling wobbly, so I got a glass of water from the kitchen (the tap water was very bitter, and not cold enough in the heat – I would have to remember to buy some bottled water to keep in the fridge) and sat down for a few minutes while I composed myself. Eventually I decided to pull myself together and abandoned my plans to unpack, deciding that going out and exploring instead might make me feel better. I took a change of clothes out of my suitcase, splashed my tear-stained face with cold water and freshened up my make-up, then headed out. By the time I left the apartment it was after 6pm, but still almost unbelievably hot and sunny, and I started to cheer up a bit. I wasn't wearing anything special, just cut-off denim shorts, a checked shirt, wedge heels, sunglasses and the Hermès bracelet I wear every day (a gold bangle covered in dark red snakeskin leather with a gold padlock charm. It was a 21st birthday gift from my mum and is a lot more tasteful and wearable than the gaudy designer jewellery she usually buys me. She did spoil it a bit by making a point of telling me that she chose it because it has 'Made in France' engraved on the side and that that's where I was conceived, and that the colour reminded her of all the red wine she'd been drinking that night. She thought that was a hilarious story to tell me), but I still noticed quite a few admiring glances, as well as some mutters of 'guapa' from men as I passed – one word I did know in Spanish. In London I probably wouldn't have attracted a second glance unless I was with Ben, but here the men were acting like they'd never seen a woman before. I decided I was going to like it here after all. I was surprised to find that all the shops were still open, but I decided to take advantage of the unexpected situation and see what Madrid had to offer. A lot of the shops I saw were the same as on UK high streets – Mango, Zara, Hoss Intropia (even a Clarks shoe shop)… – but there were also others that were new to me. I went into El Corte Inglés, a huge department store, and bought a new handbag and a bracelet from a brand called Tous that I assumed must be Spanish because I'd never come across it before. I also picked up several pretty summer dresses and a couple of tops from Bimba y Lola (a brand I knew from London and loved) without trying any of them on, as I imagined the shops must be about to close at any minute, and a pair of white hexagonal sunglasses I wasn't sure I'd ever be brave enough to wear. I never got the chance to find out the answer to that question.

When I finished shopping it was nearly 9pm and still none of the shops showed any signs of closing, which I took as another good sign that I was going to enjoy living here. I hadn't eaten since I had lunch on the plane (in first class I'd had lamb with mint sauce, carrots and dauphinoise potatoes, plus Eton mess and a cheese course so I wasn't especially hungry, but I didn't have any food at all in the apartment and I didn't know where people did their food shopping around here), so I stopped at a restaurant I passed on the way back to the apartment. I felt a bit too intimidated to go in as the place was packed with people having lively and noisy conversations, but a waiter saw me hesitating outside and waved me in. I spent a few minutes attempting to decipher the menu before admitting defeat and pointing at some unknown item, and I ended up with a kind of chickpea, pork and chorizo stew, which was actually quite delicious. I felt a bit self-conscious eating alone when everyone else seemed to be with friends or family, so I ate quickly and headed home, feeling quite proud of myself though for having eaten dinner in a restaurant not only alone, but also in a foreign country.

When I got back to the apartment and stepped into the living room, it took me a few seconds to take in what I was seeing. I stood there stunned, and only realised when I heard them fall to the floor that I must have dropped my bags. I kept blinking, probably hoping that I was imagining it and that when I opened my eyes I would see something different. All my things were strewn around the room – from where I was standing I could even see some of my clothes on the kitchen floor and worktop. Bottles of toiletries and make-up had been emptied onto the floor, and furniture and the empty containers thrown around everywhere. The books I'd brought with me had been ripped up and the crumpled pages were scattered over the floor. I don't think I had ever seen such a mess before in my life.

I couldn't understand how this could have happened... I must have been burgled, but it didn't make any sense. I'd only been out for a few hours, and it was my first day here – it didn't seem real. When I'd told my dad I was planning to come, he had warned me about getting mugged on the street and told me not to wear too many obvious designer labels that would attract the attention of thieves, but it had never even occurred to me that someone would break into my house. I didn't think anyone had even seen me moving in. It just seemed like such bad luck, and the positive impression that I had initially had of Madrid disappeared in an instant.

The mess was just unbelievable. I was walking around in a daze, picking up crumpled clothes and hanging them over my arm, when I noticed the Givenchy necklace that had been my mum's, and that she gave me on my 18th birthday. It was just lying on the floor. I wondered why the thieves hadn't taken it – even if they didn't know anything about brands, they must have been able to tell it was solid gold, and it's quite a chunky piece, which is why I never really wear it (I don't even know why I bothered bringing it with me). They would have been able to get a few hundred Euros for it just for the weight of the gold. As I wandered around puzzling over the necklace, I noticed one of my diamond earrings on the floor too, and the more I looked around, the more I came to the conclusion that they must have not taken anything at all. I couldn't decide whether to just be pleased I hadn't lost anything, or to be more worried that someone had gone to the trouble of breaking in just to make a mess. Surely if someone was going to burgle me they would have taken things rather than just throwing them around? It didn't make any sense. I didn't know what to do. I could call the police, but what would I say to them? I wouldn't be able to explain anything in Spanish, and anyway nothing was missing, so what would be the point?

I wondered what to do, and why anyone would do this. But even more than that I wondered how they had managed to do it. The door had still been locked when I arrived back, so how could anyone have got in and out? Unless they came from the patio, through the open window in the kitchen. But then the neighbours would surely have seen something if someone had scaled the wall and come in through my window. And how would they have got into the central patio anyway? They would have had to come in through one of the other apartments, unless it was one of the neighbours who had done it. The more I thought about it, the more I decided it was the only explanation that made any sense. It didn't even make sense actually, but who else could have got in? Maybe they heard I was moving in and they don't like foreign people living here. I wasn't aware of any anti-English feeling in Spain, but maybe I just hadn't heard about it – I hardly ever watch the news and I don't think

I've ever bought a newspaper in my life. Or maybe one of my neighbours just happened to be crazy – that could explain why the apartment was empty. It was plausible, but I didn't like to think that I was living in an apartment block with people who hated me, or were mentally ill – I didn't know which scenario was worse.

I went through to the kitchen and closed the window, just in case anyone had any more ideas to terrorise me, and then I sat down on the sofa holding a bundle of crumpled clothes in my arms and sobbed for the second time that day. I sobbed for a long time, not knowing what else to do. There was nobody I knew here, nobody I could phone who would come round and make it all okay. It was bad enough being alone in a foreign country and not being able to speak the language, but having all these horrible things happen too? I couldn't even phone my parents because they were on their cruise, and I would only hear from them when they were next in port, which wouldn't be for another week at least. It was just too much. I wasn't used to handling problems like this, especially in a foreign country where I had nobody to help me. But what could I do? I couldn't exactly fly straight back to London on the day I arrived and just say I didn't like it. The whole point of coming here was to prove my independence, not go running back to London and look like I couldn't survive for one day on my own. That's what I thought at the time anyway, although now I realise that

looking a bit silly would have been infinitely preferable...
Anyway, after feeling sorry for myself for a while, I started
clearing up. I hung my clothes in the wardrobe to iron
later along with the new things I had just bought, tidied
everything I could salvage into piles, and put everything
that was no longer useable into the bin.

By the time I finished clearing up it was after midnight,
and I decided to go straight to bed and just hope the next
day would be better. I didn't have any toiletries anymore
– even my toothpaste had been squeezed out onto the
floor – so I splashed my face with water, changed into a
crumpled nightdress and got into bed. I lay there for a
while, too hot to sleep – especially with no breeze coming
through from the kitchen window – and listening to the
unfamiliar noises from the other houses. There was a lot
more noise than I was used to hearing in my Chelsea
apartment, and the noise coupled with the upset of
finding the apartment in such a state meant that I felt
wide awake. I started to hear rain falling and the howling
of strong wind, a sound I had always found quite
comforting when I was warm and cosy in bed, and it made
me feel a bit better. I could almost pretend I was back in
my own bed, not in a foreign country where people broke
into my house for no reason. After lying awake for a bit
longer, I thought maybe sitting in the kitchen and
watching the rain fall would calm me down. Except that
when I went through to the kitchen, I looked out of the

window and couldn't see any rain at all. I could still hear it, but when I looked out onto the patio all I could see was a still, peaceful night. Even the leaves on the trees were moving gently, not being whipped around like I would have expected. The only explanation I could think of was that the way that the other apartments were arranged around the patio must somehow shelter it from the wind and the rain. Still, it seemed a bit odd that I could hear such a ferocious storm but couldn't see any sign of one. But what did I know about weather? I carried on wondering about it for a bit longer, then realised that I was pulling the kind of puzzled face that gives you wrinkles (my mum's "refinements" had convinced me that I never wanted any kind of cosmetic surgery, even Botox, so I've always tried not to overdo the facial expressions) so I quickly smoothed out my forehead, told myself everything was fine and went back to bed.

I hadn't been in bed for long when I became aware of another sound, apart from the rain and storm. It was faint at first, and I wondered whether it was just the wind, but it really did sound like someone crying. It was a kind of low moan with intermittent sobs. I almost managed to convince myself that it was coming from outside, and one of the neighbours had had a fight with her husband or something, but it got louder and louder until it was undeniably coming from within the room, although of course there was nobody there... It slowly started to come even closer, so that in the end it sounded as though someone was standing right next to me, crying and sobbing. Could I be imagining it? I didn't see how – I had had a long journey and it had been quite an emotionally draining day, but surely not draining enough to make me imagine something like this. I wondered whether I was asleep and it was just a dream, but normally once you question a dream, it disappears, and this didn't. And I was certain it wasn't coming from me, although it did sound like a woman. My eyes were open wide, and I scanned the dark room to try to see where the noise was coming from, but I couldn't see anything. My whole body was rigid and I realised that I was holding my breath, not wanting to make a noise. I thought that if I could just switch on the bedside lamp it would be okay, but somehow I was too afraid even to move my arm. Afraid of what, I didn't know. All I knew was that I was more afraid than I had ever been in my life, and I was completely overcome by it. I thought that if I didn't move or make any sound, maybe whatever was happening would stop. But it didn't. I was terrified, but at the same time I kept telling myself that there must be some kind of reasonable explanation for this, and it was ridiculous to be so scared. Surely if someone was in the house I'd have noticed. Unless whoever had come in earlier was still there, but why would they be crying? And where could they have been hiding all this time? I wanted to ask who was there, but my throat felt so tight, and no sound came out when I tried to speak. On the third attempt, I heard myself asking, "Who's there?" in a strained voice. No answer came, but the wailing intensified, and I started to cry again, silently, this time not brave enough even to lift my hands out from under the covers to stop the tears from dripping into my ears. My hands were shaking so much that I don't think I would have been able to control them anyway. I wanted to get out of bed and run out onto the street, but I couldn't will myself to move, and I wasn't sure my legs would be able to carry me even if I found the courage to try to escape. I was trapped alone in the dark with someone, or something, and I couldn't make it stop.

After several terrifying hours, or maybe minutes, the noise stopped, but I was still paralysed, too scared to move in case the noise – and whatever was making the noise – came back. My eyes were still staring into the darkness, and the combination of tension and fear had brought on a pounding headache. I tried to close my eyes and sleep, but it was almost painful to close them, and every time I heard even the slightest noise they snapped open again.

I can hardly believe it was possible, but somehow I must have fallen asleep, because when I woke up, it was light. I was still in the same position, and my body ached from being tense for so long, and from my fall the previous day. I hoped, and tried to believe, that maybe I had imagined it all. But my recollection was too vivid, and

I knew that it had been real. I needed to get out of this house.

Day 2

After what had happened, I couldn't stand being in the house any longer than I had to be, but my back and neck were so stiff from my fall that I struggled to get out of bed – I felt like how I imagine other people must feel when they're 90 years old. Once I managed to get up, I quickly pulled on one of my new dresses (it was lucky that I'd gone shopping really, because none of the clothes I'd brought with me were wearable), grabbed my handbag and hurried out of the house without even stopping to cut the tag out of the dress. The morning was already very warm, but the streets were quiet, so I knew it must be early. There were only a few people around – judging by their outfits, some were on their way to work and others were returning from a night out. This time there were no comments directed towards me – partly I suppose because people were too tired or too distracted with thoughts of the day ahead to notice me, but partly I'm sure because I looked like a complete hag. I was wearing no make-up apart from what was left after sleeping in yesterday's, my hair needed washing , and I must have had a crazed, wild-eyed look after what I had experienced. I found a chemist that was open and bought toothpaste, then went into a café and ordered breakfast. Or at least I thought I had ordered breakfast – I asked for it in English, adding 'por favor' as an afterthought, and the waiter nodded as though he knew what I meant but I can only imagine that he understood something completely different, because what he brought me was a plate of fried dough sticks with sugar and a cup of some kind of chocolate custard. Not that it made any difference to me what I was eating anyway because I had no appetite and I could hardly taste anything anyway. Plus my jaw ached and it hurt to chew, and I realised I must have been clenching my teeth all night.

I tried to process what had happened the night before. All I knew for sure was that someone had been in that room, and whoever it was had been crying. Except that I was alone, so there couldn't have been anyone in the room, and they couldn't have been crying. I tried to reconcile the two, but even if I was feeling fine, I don't think I'd have been able to. I tried to think of a reasonable explanation for what had happened. Was it the wind howling? It couldn't have been – it was definitely a sobbing sound. But how could there have been someone crying if there was nobody there? Unless – and even in my anxious and harassed state I knew it sounded ridiculous – it was a trick? Like someone playing a recording to try and scare me? Why anyone would want to scare me I didn't know, but it would kind of explain it. Whoever broke in and threw my things around must have planted it. Who would have done that though? I didn't know anyone here, so I didn't see how I could have any enemies, and as far as I knew nobody in the UK hated enough to follow me here to try and scare me. Maybe it was one of my dad's business rivals? I knew it wasn't a particularly realistic theory, but it was the only possibility that I could think of to explain it away instead of having to admit to myself what had really happened.

Even as I thought it I knew it wasn't true, but I just didn't know what to do. The trip that I thought would change my life for the better was already turning into a nightmare. But what could I do? I'd look so ridiculous if I just went back home. Everyone would say, 'I thought you'd moved to Madrid' when they saw me, and I'd have to say 'Oh yes, I did, but then I thought I heard crying in the night so I decided the apartment I was living in was haunted and came home the next day.' People would think I was unhinged. Looking back, being thought of as some kind of basket case would have been infinitely preferable to what has ended up happening, but at the time that's what I thought. Who's ever heard of a haunted apartment anyway? Haunted houses are big, old places in the middle of nowhere. That kind of thing doesn't happen in apartments in big cities. Or in real life for that matter. That's what I told myself, even though secretly I had always kind of believed in ghosts. My uncle once told me that when he was looking for somewhere to live, an estate agent took him to see a house that was completely unfurnished except that in one bedroom on the top floor, there was an old Victorian photograph of a woman hanging on the wall. The estate agent told them that they could do whatever they wanted with the house, as long as they never moved the picture, because whenever the picture was moved from that position, ghostly things started happening in the house. Obviously he didn't buy the house, and the story had become kind of a family joke, but I never liked talking about it because it gave me the creeps. I was curious about what exactly happened when the picture was moved, and why. And I always wondered what had happened to the last person who moved it, because it must have been pretty bad for them to tell their estate agent about it and for the estate agent to actually warn potential buyers. I wished my estate agent had done that, although I wondered whether I would have listened if they had. Only crazy people believe in ghosts, right? And maybe the estate agent didn't even know about it anyway. So there was nothing I could do but to pretend nothing had happened, forget about all the silly thoughts floating around in my mind, and just carry on as normal.

That was easier said than done. However convinced I was that I had convinced myself that everything was fine, I couldn't seem to relax. I decided that getting out of the café might help, and I was surprised when I looked up at the clock to see that I had been sitting there for nearly three hours. No wonder the waiter was glaring at me. Most of whatever it was I had managed to order had gone cold and the top of the chocolate custard had congealed, so it was even less appetizing than before. I had been so distracted by my own thoughts that I hadn't even noticed that the waiter had brought the bill. He must have been trying to drop me a hint – looking around I could see that the café was now busy. Everyone seemed so normal, talking animatedly and drinking coffee, and I thought to myself that I was being ridiculous for being scared of ghosts, because I live in the real world and ghosts don't exist in the real world – they only exist in fictional isolated villages where everyone except the protagonist is creepy and mildly insane and for nonsensical and contrived reasons they can't just move to another village where everything would be fine. I paid, leaving a €20 note for my €5.90 breakfast as an apology for tying up the table for so long. It must have worked, because as I left the waiter shouted a cheery goodbye. Well, he could have been shouting abuse for all the Spanish I knew, but even so, it sounded cheery.

I wasn't sure what to do next. I was still too nervous to go back to the apartment, but I wasn't overly keen on wandering around Madrid with no make-up and scarecrow hair. In the end vanity won, and I headed back to the apartment with trepidation, expecting to be greeted by another horrible scene but telling myself to not be so ridiculous and that everything would be fine. I unlocked the door and pushed it open all the way, peering in to check that everything seemed to be in order before taking a deep breath and stepping inside. I have no idea why I felt the need to tiptoe in and close the door softly as though I was the one who wasn't meant to be there, but I did. Everything seemed fine this time. There were no strange noises, there was no mess in the living room; everything seemed to be exactly as I had left it. I still crept around, not wanting to draw attention to my presence, and wanting to get out of there as soon as I could. Realising that I should have bought some cleanser and make-up while I was out, I grabbed the make-up I had managed to salvage the previous night, and the toothpaste I'd bought earlier, and went into the bathroom. I debated closing the bathroom door, but I was too scared that if I did, when I opened it again someone would be standing there. So I left the door open and started to get ready. I managed to brush my teeth reasonably normally, despite my hands shaking again. Then I cleaned my face as well as I could with water and started to put on my make-up. As I was applying my mascara, I went cold as behind me I thought I heard soft footsteps coming from the bedroom. Was it just my imagination? I hadn't heard them clearly, and they were so faint that they could easily have come from one of the other apartments. I stood still for a few seconds, the only movement coming from my heart pounding in my chest, then I slowly walked to the door and called out 'Hello?' in a voice I hoped would come out confidently, but actually sounded thin and weak. No answer came. I thought to myself that of course there was no answer, because nobody was there. I stood there for a few seconds but I didn't see or hear anything, so I went back to doing my make-up, telling myself that I was imagining things. I brushed my hair, then realised that because I'd been distracted I'd only put mascara on one eye. I put my hand into my make-up bag to get it out, but instead I touched something that was moving. I pulled my arm away sharply and stood for a second with my heart thumping in my chest. Now a scratching noise was coming from inside the bag, as though something wanted to get out. I knocked the bag off the side of the bath into the bath so that its contents spilled out. From among the various cosmetics, a shiny brown cockroach scuttled out and disappeared down the plughole. It was such a shock, and so disgusting that I couldn't help letting out a scream. I didn't know what to do, so I turned the hot tap on full and left it on to try and make sure it couldn't come back. It meant the rest of my make-up got soaked, but it had all been spoiled and contaminated now and I would never want to even touch any of it again, let alone use it. I shuddered when I thought that I had actually touched the cockroach – it was so sickening. I scrubbed my hands clean with soap but they still didn't feel clean. I wasn't sure they ever would. I decided I just needed to get out of the apartment, so I grabbed my handbag again and left, scanning the floor all the time on my way out in case any more cockroaches were lurking.

I ran down the stairs and breathed deeply as I opened the door onto the street. I was so glad to be out of that place. I decided to just start walking in any direction and see where I ended up. My whole body felt tense with the build-up of stress and anxiety since I had arrived, and I felt like I was in a different world from the relaxed-looking holidaymakers and locals who were wandering through the streets as though everything was fine, looking the way I used to look before I came here. I was striding quickly, unable to relax, and soon I found myself at the Prado art gallery. I'm not normally a huge art fan, but when I'd told friends that I was moving to Madrid, someone had recommended it to me, so I thought I might as well have a look. I went in and paid, and started looking around. It was huge. I didn't care which direction I went in because I was only really there to escape, not to look at paintings, so I just wandered around aimlessly. There was a school trip there having a tour in English. Even though I'd only arrived the previous day, it felt like I hadn't heard any English for weeks, and I was tempted to follow them, but if anyone realised I was following a group of fourteen-year-olds around I would look very strange, so I decided it was probably best not to, and walked in the opposite direction. I walked past lots of religious paintings and portraits of royal families and barely glanced at them. It wasn't until I got to the first floor that anything really caught my attention. Two portraits were hanging side by side — on the left was a portrait of a well-dressed, wealthy-looking woman with dark ringlets, reclining on a bed with her arms behind her head; on the right was a portrait of the same woman in the same pose, but this time completely naked. It reminded me of the pens people sometimes bring back from their holidays, the ones where you can remove the woman's clothes by tipping them upside down. I hadn't realised that people in the 1800s had that kind of sense of humour, and it made me smile for the first time in a while, more so because it reminded me of the almost life-sized nude painting of himself that Ben had in his bathroom – why would anyone do that? More to the point, why would anyone ever get involved with someone who did that... I looked to see who the artist was (of the Prado paintings, not Ben's – his didn't even look anything like him). It was Goya, and the paintings were *La maja vestida* and *La maja desnuda*. I'd heard of Goya before, but I didn't know much about him. I wouldn't have even known he was Spanish, but looking at the museum guide I'd been handed with my ticket, they seemed to have a lot of his paintings here, spread over the three floors. I imagined that his other painting might be similar, so I decided they might be worth looking at. There were lots of colourful pictures of people with parasols and things like that, but nothing especially interesting. That is, until I reached his *Black Paintings*. I don't think I'd ever seen anything like it before – grotesque images like *Saturn Devouring His Son*, which was very graphic and very disturbing – the clue's in the title I guess. But the one that most caught my attention was *The Great He-Goat* (or *The Witches' Sabbath*). It was a huge painting that took up almost the full width of the wall, and showed a group of distressed, hideous-looking women huddled together and cowering in front of their master – an imposing figure of a huge demon with horns and a cloak, who was painted completely in black in contrast to the witches' drab sepia tones. The only other character who stood out was a younger looking girl sitting in a chair. She was also dressed in black with a veil covering her head, and was perhaps about to be initiated into the group. I wondered what would make someone want to paint images like this, and I thought that Goya must have been really disturbed. I could hardly believe that this was the same man who had painted the nudes and countryside scenes I'd seen before.

I was there for quite a while, I think, mesmerised by that painting. After some time I noticed that I was quite thirsty, and that I had a headache, probably from dehydration. There was a café in the museum, but I thought some fresh air might do me good, and in any case I decided I'd had enough art for one day. In the grounds of the museum I stopped to look at the stalls selling paintings and hand-made jewellery. It was only now that I had relaxed a bit that I could appreciate the beauty of the building and its surroundings – I'd hardly noticed it at all on the way in. There were lots of tall, leafy trees – I think I had probably been expecting palm trees. I walked to a bar nearby and asked for an orange juice. It was syrupy, not like the orange juice at home, but I was thirsty and it cooled me down a bit. The bar was air-conditioned, but through the window I could see bright sunshine and people who looked like they didn't have a care in the world, and I started to think how silly I was being, thinking that anything was happening in that apartment other than someone with a twisted sense of humour playing a trick on my for some bizarre reason. There was nothing to worry about – how could there be? There was always a reasonable explanation for everything, my dad had taught me that. He had been so successful in business because he was always calm and logical, whatever the situation – especially compared to my mum, who could be counted on to be dramatic at all times. And he was always right. Well, usually right – not this time, obviously.

I didn't really feel like eating anything, so after I finished my drink and paid, I started walking again. Every time a beautiful building caught my eye, I walked towards it, and by the time I reached it I had invariably been attracted by another one. I had no idea where I was going, but after walking for a while (it seemed like hours because just moving in that heat was a struggle, but I doubt it was very long at all) I reached a lovely park. It was huge and I spent a long time there, going from one area to another and sitting down to rest on a bench before moving on again. The centrepiece of the park seemed to be a semi-circular boating lake backed by some kind of monument with statues of the main characters from *Don Quijote* –I'd read it in English as part of my degree, and found it surprisingly entertaining for something written hundreds of years ago. I'd been dreading reading it because it was so long, and I'd nearly lost the will to live reading 300 pages on the emancipation of the serfs and the harvest in *Anna Karenina*. But actually it was more like a series of short stories with the same protagonists, so it hadn't been hard-going at all. It was one of the few books I'd kept after my course ended. I wanted to take a picture, but I didn't have a camera with me and I must have left my phone at the apartment in my hurry to leave, because I couldn't find it in my bag. So I just stood and looked at it for a while, until my peace was interrupted by a young boy falling off his bike nearby. I made a move to go and help, but several people who were closer to him than I was got there first, so I decided there was no point. I was feeling sorry for him until I noticed someone subtly reaching into the handbag of one woman who had stopped to help and taking out her purse, and then catching the 'injured' boy's eye as he left with it. I have to admit I was shocked, which is probably why I didn't do anything about it. By the time I'd prepared myself to go after him he'd disappeared so it was too late to stop him, and I couldn't really go up and accuse the boy who'd pretended to fall over, because probably nobody would believe me, even if they did manage to understand what I was trying to say. Instead I just walked on, clutching my own handbag tightly under my arm.

I left the park and carried on walking for a while, but I seemed to be getting further away from the city centre and from anywhere I might want to go, so the next time I saw a sign for the underground I decided it might be my best bet. I bought a single ticket from a machine that sold it to me in English, and was amazed at how cheap it was to travel compared to London. I didn't really know which stop to go to, but looking at the map I spotted a stop called Goya, and decided it might be a good place - it seemed quite central and I recognised the name after my visit to the Prado, which I thought was probably some kind of sign. I had been bracing myself for a cramped, sweaty journey, but I was pleasantly surprised to find that not only was the whole of the underground air-conditioned, the carriages were much more spacious than any I had seen in London, although to be fair I usually took taxis so I didn't really have a huge amount of experience on the subject. I got off at Goya and found lots more shops, which suited me fine because shopping was one thing I never got bored of, especially since the shops were also air-conditioned. There was another huge *El Corte Inglés*, so I managed to amuse myself for quite a while deliberating over handbags and looking at the different Spanish cosmetic brands. I hadn't realised that Shakira had ever launched a perfume, but they seemed to have three different varieties of it on sale. There was also a Margaret Astor makeup counter, which brought back memories for me because the first lipstick my mum had ever bought me was a Margaret Astor one, called 'lilac fields' or something like that. I looked to see if they had the same one, but they didn't. The smell of the lipsticks was still the same though, and it took me back to being thirteen years old when all I had to worry about was homework and whether or not I had fallen out with whoever I had agreed to be best friends with at the time. Along with some mascara and concealer, I picked up a cheery fuchsia shade and took it to the till, for old times' sake.

When I was about to leave, I noticed a sign for a supermarket downstairs – I've always found foreign supermarkets fascinating, so I went down to see what it was like. My favourite moment was when I saw a woman buying a whole octopus in a clear plastic tub. That was certainly something I'd never seen in the Harrods Food Hall... Looking at all the food was making me hungry, so I left and looked around for somewhere I could get something to eat. There was a bar that didn't look too busy, with a sign outside advertising paella, so I went in. The paella was delicious, and I ate all of it, as well as the bread that came with it. Earlier I'd been too anxious to eat, but now that I was feeling more at ease, I realised how hungry I'd been. Apart from the waiter, there were only three other people in there – a cheerful-looking old man standing at the bar, who had nodded a greeting at me as I walked in, and who I imagined was retired and probably went there every day; and a couple sitting at a table drinking coffee – they were dressed professionally and I wondered whether they were work colleagues or a romantic couple, but it was hard to tell when I couldn't understand any of their conversation. The man looked like someone I used to know at university – a French guy who was a bit older, maybe about 40, and used to run a poetry night in a bar where anyone could go and read out what they'd written. Mostly terrible of course, but I used to go sometimes with friends from my course - just to listen, I've never written poetry. I thought he was quite a nice man, until once he invited me round for lunch and gave me pasta on a dirty plate, told me how much he disliked 'inhibited women' and then asked me to read out extracts of a pornographic novel he'd written and had (self) published in English and French while he gave me a massage. When I wasn't keen, he was annoyed and tried to get me to watch one of his films instead (all pornographic too, needless to say) so I invented an appointment I'd just remembered, to which he told me that I was lucky he was an understanding man and had so much self-control. So he wasn't so nice after all. I can be a bad judge of character sometimes. I can't remember his name though... François, maybe? Pierre? Anyway, this man was speaking Spanish, not French, so it couldn't have been him, but he did look a lot like him.

I decided it had been a bad idea to come here without learning any Spanish – I had hardly spoken a word since I arrived, and having someone to talk to would have made everything a lot easier. I had been assuming I would make friends, but I don't really know how I expected it to happen when I couldn't communicate with anyone. I suppose I thought that people would know English, or that I'd pick up Spanish. But nobody had any reason to talk to me anyway, in English or otherwise, and I couldn't pick up Spanish just by overhearing other people speaking it to each other in the street. They spoke so quickly that it was impossible to pick out words because I couldn't even tell where one word ended and the next began – it was just one really long and incomprehensible string of syllables. I decided I would need to find somewhere where I could take lessons – that would give me something to do during the day, and there'd be other people in the class who I might be able to make friends with so I wouldn't have to do everything by myself all the time. And maybe when I got quite good at it, I'd become friends with some actual Spanish people, and they'd show me all the good places to go in Madrid. Maybe we'd even go for weekends to their holiday homes in Valencia or Marbella. It would have been nice if that's how it had actually worked out.

I left the bar and set off walking again, browsing in a few shops I passed. I went into a bookshop hoping that they might sell English books, since all the books I had brought had been ruined, and I didn't have internet or television in the apartment yet and had no clue really how to go about setting them up. Luckily they did have an English-language section, although it was very small, with quite a random assortment of books. I needed something light-hearted that I could just relax with, so I chose one about a woman working as a nanny for a rich family in New York and looking for love, and another one about a woman working at a shopping channel and looking for love. They didn't seem like they would be too taxing. I thought about other things that I needed to make the apartment seem less scary and more like home, and decided that some nice candles and flowers might help, so I went on a search for them. I found candles and a vase in *El Corte Inglés* and bought a beautiful bouquet of sunset-coloured roses from a tiny florist shop, which I thought were just what I needed to brighten up the apartment.

Now that I had things to carry, I decided to get the underground back to the apartment rather than trying to find the way back on foot, which I imagined could take hours. I also picked up some takeaway McDonald's, partly because I was too tired to go out to eat, and partly because it was easy to order without any knowledge of Spanish. I took a deep breath before unlocking the door when I arrived back, and told myself to be sensible and not to let my imagination run away with me. I almost managed to convince myself that everything was fine. And it did seem fine when I got back – there was no eerie feeling and everything seemed to be exactly as I had left it, so I hoped that maybe whoever had been playing tricks on me had got bored and was going to leave me alone from now on. I put some water in the vase and arranged the flowers, then placed them on a sideboard and stood back to admire them. They really were beautiful. I was about to settle on the sofa with my book and my burger when I heard a noise coming from the bathroom. Like someone whispering. I was about to run straight back out through the door, until I remembered that I had put the hot tap on in the bath to get rid of the cockroach, and realised that I had never turned it off – that was what I could hear. I was so relieved that I laughed out loud to myself as I went towards the bathroom to turn it off. I guess I was subconsciously looking out for them because, as I passed through the bedroom, out of the corner of my eye I saw something on the chair near the bed. I held my breath and crept closer – it was another cockroach. I didn't know what to do, because I had nothing to hand that I could use to kill it, and if I started looking around for something to hit it with, I would lose sight of it and then when I looked back it might be gone. And I really wouldn't be able to stand being in the apartment knowing it was there and not knowing where it was – I'd be too scared that it might reappear at any second, and I wouldn't be able to relax. I had to kill it. I looked at it for a few seconds, trying to work out whether it had seen me. It probably had – cockroaches are supposed to be quite intelligent I think. I tried to look around the room whilst keeping one eye on the cockroach to make sure it was still there, and noticed a pile of books with half their pages ripped out that I'd picked up off the floor but not thrown out yet because I wasn't sure how recycling worked in Spain. The one on the top of the pile was a hardback. It could work. I crept slowly backwards and reached for the book while still watching the cockroach. It hadn't moved; maybe it was asleep. I took hold of the book and crept slowly towards it. I lifted up my arm, holding the book, then quickly slammed it down. Not quickly enough though, because the cockroach had worked out what I was doing and jumped out of the chair before the book landed. I could hear it scuttling across the floor as it tried to find a hiding place. I couldn't let that happen, so I chased after it and, with a bit of a leap, I managed to stamp on it. I felt the crunch as well as heard it. It was so disgusting. Afterwards I was shaking and decided I needed to sit down for a while before I went through the trauma of disposing of the body. I took my sandals off – I didn't want to wear them ever again – and went into the bathroom to wash my hands, hoping that I could wash all of this out of my mind at the same time. I remembered to turn the tap off in the bath this time too, then went back to the living room, managing not to look down at the disgusting cockroach mess on the bedroom floor as I passed it, and slumped onto the sofa. My heart was still pounding and I had lost my appetite, so I opened one of the new books I'd bought and started to read, to try and take my mind off everything. It wasn't really a very good book, but it distracted me, which is what I needed. I read for a while until I got so tired that my eyes kept trying to close, and somehow I summoned the energy to move and get into bed instead of drifting off on the sofa. I didn't even take off my make-up or change into a nightdress, I just collapsed into bed with the squashed cockroach still on the floor.

I was so exhausted, and everything seemed so calm and normal that it didn't take any time at all for me to fall asleep. I'd almost forgotten about the previous night. I started dreaming about someone crying. It took me a little while to realise I wasn't asleep, and I wasn't dreaming at all – I was actually hearing it. As much as I couldn't believe it, at the same time I think I'd always known that it would happen again. I didn't dare open my eyes. This time the crying was louder, and very close again. I was certain that if I opened my eyes I would see someone standing right next to the bed, but I couldn't bring myself to do it. I decided if I didn't move or give any indication that I was awake, maybe it would just stop again like the last time. So I listened and waited. It seemed to go on forever. I started to wonder who was crying, and why. I was too scared to try and find out though, so I kept my eyes tightly shut. And then from the other side of the room, another voice started sobbing. Then a third voice joined in, and soon it seemed as though the whole room was filled with crying and moaning. This time I really didn't know what to do. I thought to myself that I would count to ten, and if it hadn't stopped by the time I got to ten I would open my eyes. I counted slowly in my head. When I got to ten the noises hadn't stopped, so I changed it to twenty. When I got to eighteen I told myself that this time I had to just do it, so I got to twenty, held my breath and opened my eyes. I'd left the lights on when I went to bed, but they were off now – I could see shadows moving in the darkness, but I couldn't see who was making them. The crying continued. It was so loud that I couldn't think. Without realising beforehand that I was going to do it, I jumped out of bed and switched on the light, and suddenly there was silence again. I stood still for a moment, waiting for something else to happen, but nothing did.

I walked slowly and shakily into the living room and sat down. My uneaten McDonald's dinner was still in its bag on the table. I needed a glass of water. I'd forgotten to buy water, so I would have to have the bitter tap water again, but I didn't care. I took a glass from the cupboard and turned on the tap. I didn't know where the crying women had gone, and I was so worried that I would turn round and they would be there, so I was distracted, but when I looked back to the tap, I froze as I realised that the water coming out of the tap was as red as blood. I knew instantly that that's exactly what it was. I jumped back in horror and dropped the glass on the floor, where it shattered into hundreds of pieces and spilled its contents into a huge pool. Except it wasn't a pool of blood at all, just water. I turned and ran back into the living room and out of the apartment as quickly as I could. I wanted to get as far away from that place as possible. I had fallen asleep in my clothes so I was barefoot but still dressed at least. Then again, even if I had been in my nightdress I don't think I would have cared. A sign outside a pharmacy showed the time and temperature – it was 3.46am and 22 degrees. There were a few people around, going home or on to the next nightclub. I wanted to ask them for help, but I didn't know how, and I knew they wouldn't understand. I sat down on a bench and started to cry again. I must have cried myself to sleep because I woke up and I was still there, but I wasn't alone – an old, bearded man was sharing my bench, so I got up quietly and walked back to the apartment. It was light now, so nothing bad would happen. I needed to work out what to do, because I couldn't keep sleeping on public benches. Probably the only reason I hadn't been robbed was because I hadn't brought anything with me that anyone could steal. When I passed the time and temperature sign again it was 5.17am and 24 degrees. I should never have gone back, but I just didn't know what else to do, and I wasn't thinking clearly. And something was drawing me back somehow. When I arrived, the door was still ajar – I hadn't even closed it on my way out. It was light now, but I switched all of the lights back on anyway. I sat down on the sofa and hugged my knees to my chest, rocking backwards and forwards for a long time until I fell asleep again.

Day 3

It took me a few seconds when I woke up to work out where I was and remember what had happened. My heart sank as it all came back. I didn't know what to do. I couldn't stay in this apartment, but I needed to work out some sort of plan because I certainly couldn't keep sleeping on the street. It was weird - in the daytime this place didn't seem scary at all, apart from the cockroaches, but now there was no doubt in my mind that I hadn't imagined what had happened, and that something was haunting this house. It still made no sense though – why would ghosts target me? I hadn't done anything to make them angry, had I? Then it occurred to me that maybe the ghosts needed my help – people sometimes say that when you die, you can't move on if you have things you needed to do but didn't while you were alive, and that's why ghosts haunt the places where they died. And I've seen loads of films where that happens too – the characters just have to find out what the ghost wants and do it, and everything turns out fine. Maybe I just happened to move into an apartment where there were ghosts waiting for someone to arrive and help them, and maybe if I could find out who they were and what they wanted then I could stop this from happening. It was probably something simple, like in the story about the portrait that nobody was allowed to move. Maybe I'd accidentally moved something when I moved in? I couldn't think of what it could be though. But the ghosts were clearly upset about something; I just needed to work out what it was, and how to make them stop. The problem was that the only way I could think of to find out what I needed to do was to somehow ask the ghosts, but I was too scared to try and communicate, and I didn't have the first idea how to communicate with ghosts anyway, especially when they could probably only speak Spanish. Maybe I needed to find a priest and ask them to do an exorcism. Do they really happen in real life? I thought they probably didn't, but then again, a couple of days ago I had thought that ghosts probably didn't exist either. But even if I found a priest and managed to explain all this, they'd just think I was crazy, so it made more sense to me to try to help the ghosts myself so they could rest in peace. And really ghosts are just people who happen to have died, right? And most people aren't that scary. I just had to work out what to do next. I decided I would be able to think more clearly outside this apartment – I felt like the ghosts were always around here, watching me all the time.

I got dressed and ready to go out, much more calmly than the day before. I felt a bit different today – now that I'd started to think of the ghosts as just people who needed my help, instead of evil creatures who were out to get me, I wasn't so scared. I surprised myself by even being able to shower properly without jumping out every five seconds because I thought I heard something, although I was still quite worried about that cockroach coming back up through the plughole. Nothing unusual happened, and maybe even if it had I wouldn't have felt as scared as I had done before. Well, probably I would have done, but at least I was feeling slightly more confident about sorting all of this out. It's hard to believe how naïve I was just a few days ago. I really thought that all I needed to do was to solve the mystery of what the ghosts wanted from me, and then all of this would somehow be okay. Or maybe I was right, but I should have just been better at working out what it was that the ghosts wanted. Then I wouldn't be in this situation. But there's no point thinking about what I should have done differently – I can't change anything now.

I put on a navy and white striped maxi dress that I'd bought on my first day here, and left the apartment, this time walking in a different direction to before, thinking that that way I would discover more of the city. I passed more cafés, clothes shops, bakeries, a fancy dress shop... Eventually I came to an open area with various streets coming off it in every direction. It was the busiest place I'd seen so far in Madrid – there were people everywhere. Outside a bakery called *La Mallorquina* there were some buskers dressed as Native Americans playing the panpipes – not very Spanish, I thought – and lots of people were crowded around watching them. Further along, opposite a shop that seemed to sell nothing except fans – I couldn't imagine a shop like that existing anywhere other than Spain, or maybe Japan – there was a statue of someone on a horse, who I imagined must be a king, and another statue not far from it of a bear standing on its tiptoes to reach a tree. I couldn't make sense of that one at all – were bears even native to Spain? Lots of people were crowded around both the monuments; they were probably meeting friends and these were popular meeting points, although how you'd ever find anyone with three hundred people in the way was beyond me. Anyway, I quite liked the bear – it was a bit more fun than most other statues, even though I couldn't work out what it had to do with anything.

I kept on walking in a random direction. I thought I must have chosen the wrong street to go down because quite a few of the shops had obviously closed down and were boarded up with 'To Let' signs. But then I came to a busy square, with lots of people sitting outside in bars. One side of the square was taken up by a huge white building. It was so stunning that I thought it must be a palace or some kind of historical building, but it actually turned out to be a hotel. In fact I realised it was part of the same chain as a hotel that had opened quite recently near Covent Garden – I'd been to its rooftop bar before for a party and it was a really nice place with amazing views over London. I'd been meaning to go and stay there one night to see what it was like – I used to like going to London hotels sometimes, just for a night or two, because it made me feel like I was on holiday – but now I'll never have the chance. For a minute I thought I could just check in to this lovely hotel and then I wouldn't have to worry about any of these crazy problems. I had the money so why not? Whatever it cost, it would be worth it to escape from all of this. I can't remember why I can't just go there now. Maybe I just didn't think of it before. I can just go back and then everything will be fine. Oh, except I need to work out how to get out of this bed when I can't move my legs. Of course, now I remember.

I thought that if I just went and stayed in that hotel, I wouldn't have to go looking for a priest to do something about the ghosts, and I wouldn't have to tell anyone what was happening and make myself look crazy, and I wouldn't have to try and work out what was happening in that apartment and why. I could just forget about all of it and it would be as though it had never happened. I walked up the steps and through the door into the lobby. It was beautiful from the outside, and just as impressive inside, exactly the kind of place I liked staying in. I started walking towards the desk, but a powerful feeling stopped me. I felt like I couldn't just go to a hotel. I was too involved, and I needed to work out what was happening in that apartment. I'd already walked in now though, and I couldn't just turn around and walk straight back out again

– that would look really weird. Any moment now someone would come and ask if they could help me, and I wouldn't know what to say. I don't know why I was panicking about it so much, maybe just lack of sleep, but I was glad when I noticed the bar through a door on my right – I could just go there and it would look as though that's what I had come in for. I walked in and a pretty, smiley girl showed me to a booth and gave me a menu. She somehow knew where I was from and spoke to me in English. Maybe people who work in hotels get good at working out where people are from just by looking at them. Or maybe I just look really English. I don't know. Once when I was walking down the King's Road a man stopped me and just started talking to me in Russian or Polish or some language like that that I didn't understand. He didn't even ask me first whether I spoke it, so I always thought I must look Eastern European. But maybe he just didn't know any English and was going up to everyone and speaking to them in his own language and hoping that at some point someone would understand. That's what I should have done in Madrid, but how could I have known?

I ordered a drink – an orange juice that I thought might give me some nutrition since I'd hardly eaten. I was so tired and anxious that just walking around was making me feel lightheaded, but I still didn't feel in the mood for eating. The bar was basically empty, except for a man sitting on his own reading a newspaper and having a croissant and coffee for breakfast. He was wearing a suit so I assumed he was on a business trip. My dad used to go on a lot of business trips when I was younger – partly to find new ingredients or suppliers and get inspiration for new recipes when he was still more involved in running the business, and partly to spend more time with his PA, Linda, who he had an affair with for quite a few years. Really I thought my mum shouldn't have told me that, but she's never seemed too concerned about upsetting me. She was probably jealous that I've always been closer to him, and was trying to make me think less of him, but to be honest I didn't blame him – my mum's not the easiest person to put up with, and I think he struggled while I was at boarding school and they were left alone together for most of the year. I met Linda a few times. She struck me as the typical PA men always have an affair with – voluminous blonde hair with a fringe (Why do men always have affairs with women with fringes? Does it make you irresistible to men? I should have got one. Too late now though), shirts unbuttoned too low to be appropriate for the workplace, pencil skirts, patent heels, whatever jewellery my dad had bought her, five years older than his daughter. In some ways I was disappointed he didn't have more imagination, but most people do seem to live up to stereotypes I suppose. I always wondered whether she liked my dad in particular, or whether she would have had an affair with whoever her boss was if it got her some nice gifts and meant she didn't have to do much work. Anyway, she seemed like a pleasant woman whenever I met her, and at least it distracted my dad from his unhappy marriage in the same way my mum's plastic surgery and shopping addictions did for her. They've been on their cruise for about three weeks now, and I can guarantee they won't have said more than ten words to each other. I can't imagine them ever having been in love, but they must have been in the beginning I guess. That always scared me about getting married – the way people can go from being obsessed with each other to being completely indifferent, although I don't need to worry about it now. I think that's why I was always attracted to men who were indifferent to me from the start, because I didn't need to worry about them falling out of love with me if they never loved me anyway. For a while I thought I might get married to Ben. Sometimes we used to talk about it, but we'd always end up arguing because he wanted it in *Hello* so he could get more exposure, and I didn't want journalists choosing my wedding dress and forcing me to have bridesmaids from *Hollyoaks* because they don't want anyone in the pictures who isn't famous. To be honest I don't know who I would have chosen as bridesmaids – I don't have any sisters, and I've never really had that many close female friends; there are plenty of girls I see at parties or go shopping with, and I guess I'd call them friends, but I wouldn't tell them my deepest secrets or anything like that. I've never really opened up to anyone to be honest. In fact, I think this might be the most open I've ever been, which is sad. Maybe if I had had a best friend then this wouldn't have happened. I wouldn't have had to come here, or if I had it would have been with her and not on my own, and things never would have turned out like this.

I started feeling sick quite quickly. I wondered whether orange juice could make you ill. I didn't think it was likely, so I decided it must be the stress or lack of sleep - that would hardly be surprising given the circumstances. I managed to ignore it for a few minutes, but when I got that feeling in the back of my jaw, the one you get right before you vomit, I had to run to the bathroom. I was sick three times in the toilet but it didn't make me feel any better. I still felt nauseous, and I was dizzy and sweating, so I sat on the toilet floor for a few minutes until I was sure I wasn't going to be sick again and could stand up without fainting. I needed to get back to my apartment and rest – it would be fine during the day, there was nothing to worry about, and I didn't feel well enough to stay out. I went up to the bar and paid the bill, and then set off back to the apartment. I was trying to work out whether something I'd eaten had made me ill, but I couldn't even remember what I'd had to eat or when. It's so horrible being sick - I wish I could stop now, and it's even worse now because I can't move and the bed sheets are covered with it and my hair is covered with it, and I don't know how it's even possible for it to keep happening when surely there can't be anything left. The smell is just horrendous. I can hardly even bear to breathe it in, and I wish I could get away from it but it's impossible.

I managed to get back to the apartment only being sick in the street once. People looked at me as though it was my fault, but I don't know what I could have done to avoid it, and I did do it against a wall so that people wouldn't tread in it. For the first time since I'd been in Madrid, when I got back to the apartment, I was glad to be back. I lay down on the bed, and vaguely noticed that the cockroach I'd killed last night and never cleaned up had now disappeared from the floor, but I wasn't alert enough to question it. I needed a glass of water so badly, but I was confused about what had happened the night before, and anyway I wouldn't be able to get to the sink without treading on the broken glass I'd left on the floor. I wouldn't mind the broken glass now; if only I could put my feet on the floor and walk to the kitchen I would happily shred my feet to get a glass of water so I could at least swallow normally. But at that time I just wanted to rest. I closed my eyes and fell to sleep immediately. I only had one dream, about sitting on a beach somewhere in the pouring rain with one of my boarding school teachers, Mrs Cooke, who used to teach art, and she was making models out of the wet sand – really intricate things, like a man playing the piano, or two sleeping otters holding hands (they do it so that they don't drift apart – one of my favourite facts from when I was alive), even though I don't remember her being particularly good at that kind of thing – as far as I can remember all she used to do was weird things like tying shells to trees using clear thread so they looked like they were floating, but maybe that was another dream. And then I was eating the sand sculptures, and they made me feel really sick. That's what woke me up, and I ran to the toilet and was sick again. I was so tired that when I'd finished I stayed sitting on the bathroom floor and rested my head on the toilet seat. I had no energy to get up. I even closed my eyes again, but I didn't sleep this time. I had the worst headache I'd ever had up until then, probably from dehydration. I wanted to stand up and drink some water from the bathroom sink, but I was so weak that I was shaking. I closed my eyes again. When I opened them I saw something moving on the chair in the corner – another cockroach. I didn't know if it was a dream and I was just remembering when it happened before, but I was definitely awake. I needed to get up and kill it, but I just needed to rest for a little while longer. I would keep my eyes open in case it moved, and then when I felt well enough to stand up I would go and kill it, and then I would drink some water, and then I would go back to bed and rest until I was better. I watched it for some time – a few minutes I guess. It stayed still sitting on the chair. Then I told myself that the sooner I got up, the sooner I could go back to bed and the sooner I wouldn't be ill anymore. But as soon as I stood up, it ran down the side of the chair and scuttled across the floor, and disappeared into the wall. I wanted to work out where it had gone, but I didn't want to get too close and risk it touching me. I couldn't see where it could be... Maybe it had gone behind the skirting board? I couldn't just leave it there, but I needed to get back into bed. I still couldn't stand, so I crawled over to the wall. It must be somehow squished behind there, hiding in between the skirting board and the wall, so I needed something to prise off the skirting board with. I picked up a flip flop that was lying on the floor and tried to use that, even though I knew it wouldn't be strong enough, but when I went to try and lever the skirting board away from the wall, part of it just came away with no effort at all. And behind it wasn't the wall, but a gap. I made the risky move of laying my head on the floor to see if I could see it, even though I knew it could jump out at any moment and run onto my face, which was probably the worst thing I could imagine at the time. I couldn't see the cockroach, but what I could see was a pile of books. Who would put books behind a wall? It seemed so weird. I thought an old tenant must have left them there and then forgot them when they moved out. I was intrigued, so I reached into the gap and brought out the books. The cockroach was nowhere to be seen – it could be anywhere by now if it had got into the wall cavity. They were notebooks, eight of them, all different – some had hard covers and others had paper covers, they were all different colours and patterns, and some were larger than others. I opened the first one at the beginning. It seemed to be some kind of journal with handwritten notes in Spanish that went on for most of the pages. The thing that struck me as a bit odd was that the writing started off quite neatly, but as the book went on, it got messier and messier until the final pages were just a scrawl – it was impossible to even work out what most of the letters were meant to be, and the writing went almost diagonally across the page. I looked at the others, and they were all the same except the handwriting was different – eight different journals that must have been written by eight different people, and all of them just ended in a big mess. I couldn't understand what any of it meant, but even then I realised that if I could just work out what they said, these notebooks would help me work out what I needed to do to get rid of the ghosts. If only I spoke Spanish, or knew someone who did, because as hard as I tried, I couldn't make any sense of anything that was written in them. Even then I knew that these notebooks were the key to understanding what was happening in this place. I needed to get a dictionary from somewhere, and then at least I might be able to work out the key words. Then I might have a clue about what the ghosts wanted me to do, and I could just do it and the ghosts could be at peace and I could be normal and happy again. I felt like I'd already been here so long, even though this was only my third day. I couldn't even remember feeling normal or happy – maybe I never had been. Maybe it had always been like this. I couldn't remember anything anymore. I needed to talk to someone, but there was no one.

I just had to pull myself together. I knew what I needed to do: decipher the notebooks, find out what it was that would make this stop, and just do it. In some ways I felt safer having a plan, as though I could solve this and everything might work out okay. I took an empty sheet of paper from the back of one of the notebooks and started trying to work out the words from the handwriting so that I could at least make a list of words to look up once I had a dictionary. I thought maybe I could go out and get one since the shops would be open until late, but the afternoon and evening seemed to disappear and soon I found myself sitting in the dark with pages of Spanish words and no energy to leave the house and go shopping. There was nothing in the apartment that I could eat, but even though I hadn't been sick since the morning, I didn't have much appetite, and anyway the last thing I wanted was to eat and then be ill all night. I was too tired anyway, and even though I knew what might happen, for some reason I thought that now that I'd found the notebooks and it seemed as though I was starting to make progress on solving everything, the ghosts might realise I was on their side and trying to help them. Then maybe they'd leave me alone.

As I tried to sleep, I told myself that it was fine, that the ghosts wouldn't harm me, and even if they were crying it would just be because they were unhappy and needed my help – it wasn't the ghosts' fault, they weren't trying to frighten me. That's what I was trying to convince myself – I didn't realise how wrong I was. So I was prepared for the ghostly crying. But still every sound I heard startled me and made me jump, and there was no way I could drift off to sleep. I don't know how much time passed, but while I was still lying there with my eyes closed, I sensed someone – obviously a ghost – walk towards me and stand next to my bed, then lean over and start whispering to me in Spanish. I couldn't understand any of it, but she was whispering in an urgent tone, as though she was desperate to tell me something. Why didn't I learn Spanish before I came here? I was so stupid. The Spanish started as a whisper, and then got louder and louder until she was screaming into my ear. I was terrified – I wanted to open my eyes and sit up and try to speak to her and tell her to stop. Why couldn't I? I just lay there and did nothing. And then more voices joined in. More ghosts. All of them were women's voices, screaming at me, and all in Spanish. I couldn't think or hear anything except their shrieks filling my head. Couldn't the neighbours hear this? Wouldn't one of them come to help? But I knew nobody would. I was on my own, just like now. I don't know if I even have neighbours – I never met any of them. Maybe I'm the only one here. Well, not the only one. I thought in that moment when the screaming was so loud and so terrifying, that it must be possible to actually die of fear, and that maybe my heart would just stop beating and I'd die, like the JLS song that I've had stuck in my head for days or maybe just hours, but from terror instead of heartbreak. Maybe heartbreak too. Somehow it didn't stop beating though. Maybe it would have been better if it had just stopped then. I knew that all I needed to do was reach out and switch on the light and all of it would end, like every other time. But like every other time I couldn't. I just needed to find that little bit of courage. But all the screaming was in my head and I couldn't think and I didn't know what to do. But then somehow without even knowing I was going to do it, I did do it. The screaming suddenly stopped of course and now all I could hear was my heart beating. But I was okay, it was over. That's what I thought anyway until I saw something red out of the corner of my eye – I turned to look at the wall right above my bed, and I saw it, written in red in huge letters: VETE. What could it mean? I realised that I'd been lying to myself about how scared I really was. And I was silly to think I could sort all of this out myself. I couldn't help these ghosts and I couldn't stop what they were doing and I couldn't stay here. I had to get out.

I quickly grabbed some things and ran out of there. I knew I could go back to the hotel I saw earlier – I just needed to find it again and I still didn't know the city. I thought I might be able to remember the route I'd taken that morning, but I realised I'd made a wrong turn somewhere when I found myself on a street I definitely hadn't seen before. It was full of bars and clubs and people. A man approached me – he was obviously Latin American with soft features, thick, curly black hair and dark eyes. Maybe he would help me. He said something in Spanish and handed me a card for a bar called Cibeles that I could see further down the street. Then he looked at me as though maybe somehow he understood everything I was feeling, even though I didn't even understand everything I was feeling and I wanted so much to speak to him and explain everything but I just smiled and he smiled back with the kindest smile I'd seen since I arrived here and maybe ever, and walked away. I turned and walked back down the street and I was crying, maybe because it was the first time someone had been kind to me since I got here, and I really more than anything just needed someone like him to be kind to me and let me tell him everything that had happened to me – even if he didn't know what I was saying, it wouldn't make a difference. But I'd missed my chance. I just had to find the hotel though and I'd be fine. After a little while I recognised the street I should have gone down, and I found my way back to the square and the hotel.

In contrast to the busy square, when I walked into the hotel there was no one in the lobby except the man at the reception desk. I asked him for a room, and when he asked how many nights I would be staying for I didn't know what to tell him. I hadn't thought about what I was going to do, but maybe I could just stay until I decided whether to look for a different apartment or just go straight back to London. I told him a week or maybe longer. He was either so professional or uninterested that he didn't even look surprised at the vagueness of my answer or lack of luggage, and after getting me to fill out the usual forms he gave me the key to my room on the second floor. When I opened the door to my room, I stepped in and immediately felt better. Even the smell was reassuring, and I knew I was safe now. I couldn't understand how I could go from being so scared such a short time ago to feeling almost relaxed – it was like suddenly being in the real world, and the apartment and everything that happened there was just a bad dream. I sat down on the beautiful bed and knew that I could close my eyes here and sleep and not worry about anything. After so long without resting, I wasn't sure when I would wake up, so I hung the 'do not disturb' sign on the door. This was what I was used to – a comfortable bed, attractive surroundings, soft towels and expensive toiletries in the bathroom. This was my life. Not the other one. And I wouldn't go back there.

I switched on the TV, just for noise really since I'd had nobody to speak to for so long. A man who looked like a Spanish Louis Theroux was going up to random people in the street and speaking to them, and somehow the woman walking around with him seemed to be winning money, or trying to win money. I would have thought game shows would be the easiest kind of programmes to understand in a foreign language, but I couldn't work it out. The contestants kept changing and I couldn't tell whether they'd won anything. I changed the channel and found something that seemed to be a bit like the *X Factor*, or maybe *Stars in Their Eyes*. There was a middle-aged man dressed up as a schoolboy with painted-on freckles, shorts and a rucksack, singing something in Spanish and apparently trying to sound like a child. I couldn't really make much sense of this programme either, because surely he'd stand a better chance of winning if he tried to sound like someone who was at least an adult. The next woman was singing an old Motown song, except that instead of the *Age of Aquarius* she was singing about the *Age of Aquarium*... Not that I'd be able to sing Spanish lyrics correctly, but it still made me laugh, although maybe I was just a bit hysterical. It was so bizarre but the normal kind of bizarre if that makes sense – the kind of bizarre that happens in real life, not the kind that only happens in horror films. Anyway, it was at least entertaining.

Now that I didn't have that anxious feeling anymore I was quite hungry, so I took some crisps from the mini bar while I looked at the room service menu. Luckily there was an English translation, so I didn't have to worry about accidentally ordering pigs' ears or anything. I rang down and ordered ham croquets, olives, bread and chorizo. I was excited about my mini buffet. I once had a business idea for a 'buffet for one' – I thought it seemed unfair that people who live alone can't take advantage of *M&S* mini party food because, really, who wants to eat 12 mini duck spring rolls to themself? The whole point of party food is to have a variety. So wouldn't it be good if you could buy a one-person buffet with a couple of spring rolls, smoked salmon blinis, mini quiches, that kind of thing? I think the Dragons might have liked it, but they always want business plans and things. I can only do ideas. And anyway, people might be too embarrassed to buy something that clearly tells the person at the till that they are single and going to pretend to themselves that they're at a party when really they're just at home on their own. They could always go to the self-service till I suppose, then they wouldn't have to be embarrassed. Although I'm sure it won't be long until technology evolves so that the annoying "unidentified item in bagging area" woman starts being able to comment on people's purchases.

The food arrived quickly, and I ate it sitting cross-legged on the bed while someone who was dressed as Shakira but who was clearly male, sang *Whenever, Wherever* in Spanish. He even did the yodelling part, and the audience seemed to love the whole performance, especially the belly dancing. I didn't know what the judges were saying, but the Shakira man seemed happy so it must have been positive. Maybe the Spanish just have really unusual taste in entertainment. I wondered whether the format would make it to the UK. I couldn't really imagine it. Actually though, I think I might have seen an advert for something like it on ITV, although I thought that surely people in the UK wouldn't watch anything like this. Anyway, the food was delicious, and it made me feel full and warm and sleepy. The best thing was I knew I could sleep here and everything would be fine. I smiled to myself – the truest kind of smile I sometimes think, when there's nobody else around – and laid back on the bed. I just wanted to sleep. I didn't even want to get undressed or brush my teeth, but I eventually persuaded myself to get up, and I got ready for bed in my beautiful bedroom. Then I settled into bed and confused myself trying to turn off the lights – there were so many switches, and at one point I accidentally turned on pink lighting, which was quite fun but not really what I was aiming for. Eventually I managed to turn off all the lights except the one by the door, which I left on just in case – I felt safer, but not that much safer – and soon I felt myself falling asleep.

I didn't wake up until the morning. Bright sunshine was coming through the gap in the curtains, and I opened them and looked down onto the square. It was busy with people. I had expected that I would probably sleep for at least 12 hours, but it was only 9.30. I felt so rested compared with just a few hours ago. I decided to have a bath, and wondered whether the hotel had a spa. That would be wonderful – I could have a massage and start to properly relax and get back to normal. The bath was huge, and the toiletries were lovely. I stayed in there for ages, starting to feel like the old me again. Now all I needed was to meet some friends for lunch and shopping and I'd be back to real life. Even though I didn't feel scared anymore, and as far as I knew I no longer had any reason to worry about any of this, I still felt so lonely. I'd hardly spoken to anyone for days, and when I had, it was a couple of words here and there. I thought I might have forgotten how to even have a conversation, it had been so long. I thought about the man from last night and that I should have talked to him, but there was no point dwelling on past mistakes. Anyway, it definitely seemed like things would be fine now. And they would have been if I'd just stayed there. I should have stayed in that room and never left, and got them to bring me my food and watched those bizarre TV programmes and I should have never stepped out of that hotel where everything was okay and I didn't need to be scared. I thought I would stay. I thought I would never come back to this apartment – I didn't need to, and why would I after everything that had happened to me here? I didn't know that I would come back, and that this time I would never be able to leave again.

Day 4

I sat around the room most of the morning. It was such a nice change to not feel as though I needed to rush out as soon as I could to escape from whatever had been terrorising me since I arrived in Madrid. I switched on the television again, but whatever was on seemed to be mainly people shouting at each other, so I switched over and found very similar programmes on most of the channels. Eventually I settled on some kind of news programme, which was at least a bit calmer. I ordered scrambled eggs and croissants from room service and ate my breakfast with the window open, looking out over the square. It was another beautiful sunny day in Madrid, and everyone I could see seemed to be enjoying the day. I decided I should do the same, but first I needed to make myself presentable. I'd hardly brought anything with me, so I would have to wear the same dress and underwear again. Probably nobody would know the difference, but I realised I would need to go out and buy some more new things if I was going to avoid having to go back to the apartment. I'd just left my hair to dry naturally after my bath so it was nicely wavy but with a bit too much frizz. I should have had my roots done before I left for Spain too, but my usual stylist was on maternity leave and I was nervous about going to anyone new after a bad experience when I went to a random stylist at *Headmasters* who asked what I wanted and then told me no, I didn't want a trim, and that he knew exactly what to do to make me look amazing. I personally wouldn't have said that the asymmetrical bob with micro-fringe did much to make me look "amazing", and considering that it was the first and only time I appeared in *Heat* magazine's 'What Were You Thinking?' page ("Did socialite Milly Somerville get that haircut free with the pack of tin foil she fashioned into a skirt?"), I wasn't the only one. After that I didn't really like going to high street salons, and everywhere else gets booked up months in advance, so I had decided the roots would just have to wait. Anyway, maybe this was kind of Coachella chic. I did what I could with the comb in the bathroom, and put on the Margaret Astor lipstick I'd bought the other day that luckily was in my bag. I wasn't overly impressed with what I saw when I looked in the mirror, but it was the best I could do until I managed to get some supplies. I looked down at my hands and noticed what a mess my nails were. I'd had a manicure before I left London, but now it was chipped and my nails were ragged from biting them – I hadn't even noticed I'd been doing it, but it was hardly surprising. I rang down to reception and asked if they could bring a nail file up for me, and a small and cheerful man who was starting to go prematurely bald arrived at the door with it within about two minutes. I tidied my nails as much as I could, but with the chipped nail polish they still looked awful. They would just have to wait until I got to a shop though; nobody would notice or care about my nails anyway. It's just that I felt as though now I was starting to feel better, I ought to look better too.

When I left the hotel the sun was blinding. I looked in my bag for my sunglasses but they weren't there – I must have lost them somewhere. It was fine though, I would just have to get some more. I decided to go back to *El Corte Inglés* – I thought they'd have everything I needed, and I still didn't really know many other shops. I found some pretty, pale pink sunglasses that were more normal than the ones I'd bought as an impulse purchase a couple of days earlier and abandoned at the apartment with almost everything else. Then I went upstairs and walked around just picking up clothes I liked – I wasn't really in the mood for trying anything on. I ended up with four large carrier bags - luckily they accepted Amex. I'd been planning to go to *Zara* and *Mango* too, but I had too much to carry so I just headed back to the hotel, then remembered to stop at *Sephora* on the way to buy concealer to cover up the dark circles that now looked like they had been tattooed onto my face by a disgruntled tattoo artist. I got some blusher and mascara, thinking that now I would at least look human. I knew I was wasting money buying the same things over and over, but money was one thing that wasn't a problem for me, and if it meant I didn't have to go to the apartment then it was fine with me. When I was about to leave, I saw the perfume wall and thought that some new perfume might

72

be exactly what I needed to help pick up my mood. I smelled a few and chose the most cheerful, summery, uplifting one I could find, since that was how I was determined to feel. Then I remembered that I didn't have any basic toiletries either, apart from the free ones in the hotel, so I quickly picked up deodorant and some cleanser and moisturiser, plus some nail polish remover and a new bright pink polish so I could sort out my nails. Then I carried everything back to the hotel, excited to try on my new purchases.

Once I had put on my new dandelion print playsuit and painted my nails, I felt almost like any normal girl on holiday. There was only one thing that had started to nag at me slightly – those notebooks, and that message on the wall. I hadn't thought to bring the notebooks with me last night, but in my bag I had the sheets of paper with the words I thought I could check in the dictionary. And there was still that writing on the wall that I couldn't figure out – VETE… If I bought a dictionary, maybe I'd have a chance of understanding what had been going on in the apartment without actually having to go back there. I didn't know why I was even thinking about it, but I felt a kind of compulsion to understand what had happened to me and why. And I guess part of me still thought that I might be able to resolve whatever was going on there, even though I told myself I just wanted to forget about it completely.

I tried to find my way back to the bookshop I'd been to before, but found the *El Corte Inglés* bookshop first, so I went in and bought a pocket English-Spanish dictionary, which I was sure would tell me what I needed to know. I went straight back to the hotel room to start my investigation. I immediately hit a problem though, as I found that 'vete' – the main word I wanted to look up, and the one I thought was the key to understanding the haunting – didn't appear in the dictionary at all. I was confused, but when I thought about it more I decided that that must mean that either it wasn't a Spanish word at all (I didn't know what it could be otherwise though – maybe Latin or something? For all I knew the ghost could have been talking in Latin too – I just assumed it was Spanish because it wasn't English and I was in Spain), or it was some kind of acronym, in which case I would have almost no chance of finding out what it meant, especially since I still hadn't found my phone so I had no internet. I never did find it. Now I realise that I just didn't understand how dictionaries work, or I wasn't thinking straight, I don't know which. Maybe both. It's really hard to concentrate now, and sometimes I can't remember if I'm telling everything in the right order, or if I'm even telling the right things at all or I'm imagining things or dreaming them, but I have to try. It's so hard though, especially with this pain. Anyway, I remember looking in the dictionary and I remember that I couldn't find that word. I tried looking up some more words, but without full sentences they made no sense. I decided it was no use and I should just drop it. I should have just dropped it. Why didn't I?

I was frustrated after getting nowhere trying to work out the Spanish, so I decided to go for a walk and get some air and sunshine to clear my head. I asked in reception again about the Royal Palace – I knew there was one somewhere in Madrid, but so far I hadn't seen it, even with all the walking around I'd been doing. The receptionist gave me directions and told me it would take 20 minutes or so to walk there. He said that the walk would take me through the Plaza Mayor, which I thought might be nice since I hadn't seen that yet either. He also told me that next door to the palace was a cathedral called the Almudena that was free to visit. I set off walking and found the Plaza Mayor quite easily. As soon as I stepped into the square I decided that it t was my favourite place in Madrid – it was so busy and vibrant with people sitting outside bars and restaurants all around the square, others sitting with their friends on the floor, and some even lying down and sunbathing. There were also various artists selling oil paintings or offering to draw caricatures, and an Asian man holding a sign that said "masajes 5€" which I realised must mean that he was offering massages, but I still pretended not to understand when he came up to me – I realised that was a mistake when he proceeded to demonstrate what he meant by pinching me in the back with some kind of Vulcan death grip manoeuvre that gave my whole back pins and needles, while repeating 'masaje, masaje'. I managed to get away, but I was quite shaken up, mostly because I wasn't expecting him to just grab me, and also because if he could make my whole back go numb instantly then he could probably kill me in half a second if he wanted to. I was just overreacting because I was still so tense, even though I had been thinking that I was fine now. I walked away as quickly as I could, looking behind me every few seconds just in case he was following me, but he was already busy with his next potential victim.

I felt better once I was back onto the street, and I soon arrived at the palace. It was beautiful — much nicer than Buckingham Palace I thought, and I loved the blue colour, although it could have done with a steam clean because it looked a bit grubby close up. I debated going inside, but decided that I wasn't really in the mood for traipsing round with an audio guide, so I walked around the grounds and found a bench in the shade to sit on. There were people around, and a busker with a guitar singing what I thought must be flamenco or Spanish folk songs, but it was still much calmer than many of the other places I'd been to in Madrid. I sat for a while and then I decided to go and get lunch somewhere, but then I passed a big church, and I realised that this must be the cathedral the receptionist at the hotel had mentioned. I don't really know why I went in or what I was hoping would happen. I hadn't been in a church for years. Not since I was little and I was a flower girl at the wedding of the daughter of one of my dad's business associates. I didn't 100% realise it at the time, but she was clearly crazy, and I still can't work out why her parents went along with her Renaissance theme. If it had just been the outfits it wouldn't have been so bad – although wearing a green velvet cloak and pointed hat at seven years old wasn't my finest fashion moment – but dressing horses up as unicorns was just taking it too far. I always thought that my wedding would be much more classy and elegant, but we'll never know now. I'd always envisioned something small and intimate, maybe on a beach somewhere, but in reality I'm sure it would have been a nightmare because my mum would have insisted on it being the biggest, flashiest wedding anyone had ever been to. She would have invited hundreds of guests – most of whom I probably never would have even met before – and hired Beyoncé or Lady Gaga or someone to perform, so that in the end no one would have noticed I was even there. I would have hated it, but I still wish I'd had the chance. Whatever had happened it would be better than being here, writing this and waiting to die, even hoping to die.

There are so many things I'll never do now – things I always assumed I would do one day. Like having a baby. I've never really wanted a baby, but I imagined I'd have one eventually. I know my dad would have loved a grandchild, although he never would have put any pressure on me. And my mum would have liked it too I think, although mainly so she'd have an excuse to buy more things. Even having a job is something I'll never do. Just having a column in *Tatler* or something would have at least given people a reason to respect me, and then I would have had my own money instead of just relying on my dad. I never read James Joyce's *Ulysses* either – I was supposed to read it for my degree but it was around the time of the university fashion show that I was modelling in and helping to organise, so I was busy with that (it seemed like a sensible priority considering that Kate Middleton managed to attract Prince William at a university fashion show just by modelling in her underwear) and I read a summary instead. I thought I would read it another time, but I never did. There are too many things to even think of. Learn Spanish, of course. If I'd learned Spanish before I came here then I wouldn't even be writing this, and I could do all these things and more. What's the point of thinking about that though – I just need to finish telling this story. That's all I can do now.

I always thought of churches as being dark, but this one was bright, with colourful stained glass windows that cast pretty shadows everywhere. I sat down on a seat facing the front. It was quiet, peaceful. There was a tiny old lady kneeling in front of an altar, gazing up at a figure of a dying Jesus on the cross that was hanging on the wall. She was praying out loud, and seemed oblivious to the other people walking around her. I heard movement on my right, and turned round to see what was happening. There was a man in a suit lighting a candle; his head was bowed and he seemed to be concentrating intensely. I wondered who the candle was for. He stood there for a minute or so as though he was saying a silent prayer, then he sat down just a few seats away from me. I couldn't tell for sure, but I thought he might be crying. I tried to look at him out of the corner of my eye so that it wouldn't be too obvious, but I couldn't see him properly without looking at him directly, and I didn't want him to know that I was looking at him. Regardless of whether or not he was crying, from what I could tell he seemed seriously good-looking – dark hair and handsome features. I thought to myself that it's probably not okay to look at men in that way in a church, but I couldn't help it. Without realising it, I'd turned to look at him face on, and he looked up and caught me staring at him. I quickly looked away, but when I glanced back, he was smiling at me. If he had been crying before, he definitely wasn't now. He whispered "hello" in English with a slight accent, and asked me what my name was. I told him, and he said that it was a pretty name and that it suited me, which made me blush. I couldn't believe I was flirting with someone in a church. He told me his name was Julián - I'd never heard the name before, but it sounded beautiful when he said it. He said that we should go outside so that we could talk properly. I've always liked men who are confident like that. I stood up and so did he, and we left the cathedral and stood outside. The more I looked at him, the more I realised how attractive he was – he was tall, a good few inches taller than my 5'7", with broad shoulders, dark hair, and dark skin. He was the typical tall, dark and handsome man that people talk about I guess, except that his eyes were a clear, pale blue. They would have been striking even in the UK, but I couldn't remember having seen anyone with anything other than brown eyes since I arrived here. I tried not to stare, but there was something mesmerising about him. I even felt as though I kind of recognised him somehow. For some reason I thought about when I was still in London and imagining my life in Spain, and I remembered my crazy fantasy about meeting a Spanish bullfighter and having a great romance. Apart from the eyes, he looked exactly like the man I would have imagined if I had a better imagination – maybe that's why I felt as though I'd seen him before. I asked him how he knew I spoke English, and he said that he just knew. I hadn't been this attracted to anyone for a long time. He asked me if I was a vegetarian, which I thought was a weird question. I told him I wasn't, and asked why he wanted to know. He said it was because one of his favourite restaurants in Madrid was a vegetarian restaurant nearby and that he'd like to take me there for lunch. I tried to suppress a smile, and said that it sounded lovely and I'd love to go with him. He looked pleased when I agreed, and I couldn't help being pleased too. Suddenly things were starting to happen the way I'd wanted them to when I came here. I hadn't been on a date for at least a couple of years, since before I met Ben, and I felt uncharacteristically nervous. I'd just been planning to spend the day sightseeing alone, so I wasn't prepared for this at all. He led the way, and we crossed the road and then soon afterwards we started going down steps that I hadn't even noticed when I walked past earlier, and I could see that there were other streets below where I had been, as though a completely new city existed underneath the one I'd been in until now. We hadn't walked for long when we came to a picturesque small square – there were a couple of restaurants and some people sitting outside, and we went into a restaurant on our right. Julián said that he preferred to sit inside where it was quieter and we could talk properly. It was also air-conditioned, which would be a welcome break for me from the oppressive heat.

We were shown to a table upstairs, which was on a kind of mezzanine looking down over the rest of the restaurant. It was a fairly small place, and very cute – it had old-fashioned wooden chairs, all the tables had blue and white checked tablecloths, and there were blue and white tiles on the walls. I loved places like this - it almost reminded me of a French bistro, except the fans hanging from the walls made it obvious we were in Spain. Julián asked if I'd like him to order for me, and for some reason I said yes. I don't know why - I usually get a bit funny about men ordering for me (I had a bad experience at university when a guy I met in the gym took me out to a Moroccan restaurant on a date and ordered tap water and one main course between us to share – I like to think that I'm not a snob, and I get that not everyone's dad is in the Rich List, but he insisted he was going to pay for everything even though I had said I was happy to pay half, so if he didn't have the money then maybe he just should have invited me out for a drink or coffee or even just a walk rather than dinner. It was just awkward, and then he made it a million times worse by complaining to the waiter that there wasn't enough food. If that had been the worst part, it wouldn't have been so bad, but the fact that every time he spoke to the waiter he put on a fake Moroccan accent and called him 'Habib 'made it one of the most embarrassing nights of my life, and definitely one of the worst dates I've ever been on). Anyway, for some reason with Julián I didn't mind – I guess I instinctively trusted him, and anyway the alternative was looking at a menu in Spanish and ordering something at random, so either way I wouldn't really be choosing for myself. The waitress came over and he spoke to her in rapid Spanish, and then as soon as she had gone he started talking to me in English again. I was amazed at how he could just switch from one language to the other so effortlessly. I asked him why his English was so good, and he told me that he'd learned English as a child, but that he was more interested in finding out about me. He asked me how I'd ended up in Madrid, and even though I usually follow the standard rule of never talking about ex-boyfriends on a first date, for some reason I found myself telling him all about Ben and how he'd broken up with me, and I even for some reason told him about the time Ben hit me when he said that I'd embarrassed him in front of a director at a party and he thought that because of that he had missed out on getting a part he wanted. I'd never told anyone that before, ever in my life – even with Ben we'd never talked about it or even acknowledged that it had happened. It was almost as though I wasn't in control of what I was saying, and everything was just spilling out of me – not just emotions I'd been keeping inside for the past few days, but for years.

The starter arrived and Julián explained that it was pumpkin soup, but cold like gazpacho, with a scoop of cold mashed potato and sweetcorn. It sounded disgusting, and I was slightly regretting agreeing to Julián ordering, but he most have seen my face and told me to trust him and that I would love it. And I did - it was one of the most delicious things I'd ever eaten. I could hardly believe it. I told him it was amazing and he just smiled. He said that I had to promise from now on that I wouldn't doubt him again, and I promised. I felt like I'd been talking so much and I still didn't know anything about him at all, even what his job was, so I asked him what he did for a living. He told me that he had his own business, but before I could ask him any more about it, the main course arrived. It was rice, plantain, ratatouille, fried egg and salad – Julián said it was a Cuban dish. I've been to Cuban restaurants before in London and New York, and I always thought Cuban food was mainly meat and seafood, but this was wonderful – Julián had made a brilliant choice again, and I decided that I really ought to trust him like he said.

I didn't want to tell Julián about the ghosts, but he asked me whether I was planning to stay in Madrid for long, and I just burst into tears at the table. I've never been a particularly emotional person, and certainly crying in the middle of a restaurant on a first date with a man I've known for an hour is not my usual style, but everything felt different with Julián. He had some kind of effect on me and I felt not just that I could tell him anything, but that I wasn't capable of hiding anything from him at all. He didn't even seem surprised that I was crying – nothing seemed to surprise him – he just reached over and put his hand on top of mine, and I realised it was the first time anyone had touched me since I'd been here. He had a concerned look on his face, and I thought that maybe at last someone here actually cared about me. He asked me what was wrong, and I told him that he wouldn't believe me if I told him and he'd think I was crazy, and he told me that I had promised to trust him, and he promised to believe me too. So I told him everything – the luggage being thrown around, the crying in the night, the notebooks, sleeping on the street, the cryptic message on the wall, all of it. I thought he'd laugh, or just get up and walk straight out of the restaurant, but he looked me straight in the eye with those piercing blue eyes of his and told me he believed me. I thought he must be joking but the way he was looking at me told me he was serious. I told him I was surprised that anyone could believe it, because I wouldn't have believed it myself a week ago, and I asked him why he was so sure I was telling the truth. He held my gaze and said: "There are more things in heaven and earth, Horatio, than are dreamt of in your philosophy." I had never been on a date before with a man who quoted Shakespeare to me, let alone when English wasn't even his first language, and I found it ridiculously romantic. I was elated that after going through all of these horrors alone, finally someone was listening to me and understood. And when that someone just happened to be a gorgeous and intelligent man who seemed to really like me, even better. It was beyond a dream, and when I remembered how awful I had felt just the day before it seemed unbelievable.

He asked me if I needed to go back to the apartment to get my things, since I'd told him how I'd rushed out the night before with hardly anything, but I said no, I never wanted to go back there, I just wanted to pretend I had never been there at all, and if whoever cleaned the apartment for the next unfortunate tenant wanted to take my clothes then that was fine with me. Then I remembered the notebooks, and I thought that maybe Julián could tell me what they meant. But I told myself that they didn't matter now, and I just needed to leave all of that behind me. He must have been able to tell that something was on my mind because he asked me what was wrong. I told him – I just couldn't seem to stop myself – and he said that of course he would tell me what they meant if it would give me some kind of closure, and asked whether I would feel okay about going back to the apartment if he was with me. He promised that no ghosts would harm me if he was there. I believed him, I don't know why, but I should have trusted my instincts and never come back here. I just thought to myself that maybe it would be fine if he was with me, because I wouldn't be scared, and if I wasn't scared than those ghosts couldn't have any power over me. I said yes, but that I wasn't sure I was ready to go back there yet, and he smiled and said that that was fine because we still hadn't had dessert. It wasn't even funny, but it made me laugh just because he was so charming. I couldn't even remember the last time I'd laughed so much. I felt like I was really letting go at last, and that maybe I was going to enjoy Madrid after all.

The waitress brought our desserts, and when she put my plate down she looked at Julián and then caught my eye and gave me a knowing smile. He was a very good-looking man, so it wasn't surprising that we were attracting attention. The dessert was layers of pastry and ricotta cheese with red berries and honey, and it was so lovely that I thought I would try making it myself at some point. Julián didn't seem surprised when I told him I was very impressed by his choice of restaurant. He asked if I was ready to go back to the apartment, and I said I wasn't sure. He told me not to worry because he would be with me, and I thought that he was right, and that I didn't need to worry if he was there. He also said that it was better that we went now, in the daytime, so that we could be gone before it got dark since that was when anything strange might happen. It seemed to make sense. I still wasn't sure I wanted to go back again, but at least this way I could pick up the notebooks and find out what they said. Julián left some cash on the table to cover the bill, and then we left the restaurant and walked out into the sunshine. We took a different route from the way we'd come, walking uphill on tiny back streets until we suddenly arrived back at the Plaza Mayor. On the way back to the house, we passed someone I recognised – the guy who had given me the flyer the day before. He didn't notice me, probably because he was with a beautiful woman with an amazing figure and long, dark, wavy hair. They were clearly together – they couldn't seem to take their eyes off each other – but it didn't matter now, because I had Julián and he was going to help to make everything okay. When we were walking, I remembered that I had thought he might have been crying in the cathedral, and I asked him who he had been lighting a candle for. He said that it was for his girlfriend who had died, but that he didn't want to talk about it yet because it wasn't the right time. I wanted to know more, but decided not to push it because I didn't want to upset him. I thought how tragic it must have been for him to lose someone he was in love with, and wondered whether she had been ill or whether it had been some kind of accident. It must have been awful for him. Maybe that's why he'd been so understanding about what had happened to me.

We arrived at the apartment and I couldn't help shivering as I walked through the door, but everything seemed quiet and still. It struck me as an eerie stillness rather than a peaceful one, but that was no surprise after what had happened here, and I thought that it wouldn't matter anyway because I would be gone soon, and this time forever. Well, I was certainly right about that, but not in the way I thought. We went into the living room and sat down. I couldn't offer him anything to drink but it wouldn't matter if we weren't going to be here for long. I meant to just get the notebooks straight away so that we could leave, but somehow we started talking – Julián asked me some question that I can't even remember, and before I knew it I was talking about my mum and dad, growing up, even telling him things I had completely forgotten up until that moment, like Stephanie Maitland from the year above hiding spiders in my bed when I was at boarding school, and all the other girls laughing at me when I screamed.

Somehow hours must have passed – I only noticed how dark it had become when Julián got up to switch on the lights. We had been talking for so long – I had anyway – and I suddenly felt exhausted. I told Julián that I needed to get back to the hotel, and we could take the notebooks with us and look at them tomorrow. I was almost too tired even to go through to the bedroom to get them – I couldn't work out what was wrong with me. I went through and picked them up, and when I handed them to Julián he opened the first one and started to read it silently. I didn't want to interrupt him, but after a few minutes he still hadn't said anything and I was so desperate to know what was in them, as well as to get back to the hotel so that I could sleep, that I had to stop him to ask if he had found anything. He said that he needed to read to the end before he could really understand what it was about, and that I needed to sleep but he would read them overnight and then in the morning we could talk about what they said. I wanted to go back to the hotel, but I was so tired and Julián suggested that I could just sleep here and he would make sure nothing happened. He said that he wouldn't sleep anyway because he'd be reading the notebooks, so I didn't need to worry about anything happening. Maybe I was just too tired to argue, or maybe I really did trust him that things would be fine, but I got straight into bed and before I knew it I was asleep.

Day 5

When I woke up I didn't know where I was for a second. I rubbed my eyes sleepily, then my heart froze when I realised that I was back in the apartment, and I immediately sat up in bed in a panic. But then I saw Julián sitting in the chair next to the bed and smiling at me and I was so relieved when I remembered what had happened. He must have been sitting there all night. I smiled at him and he said hello and asked me how I'd slept. I said I'd slept really well but that he must have been uncomfortable trying to sleep sitting up in that chair, and he said that it didn't matter because he didn't need to sleep, he just wanted to look after me and make sure I was okay. I said that after everything I'd been through here before, I couldn't believe that nothing had happened in the night, and he replied that of course nothing had happened because he'd been here. I still didn't realise how true that was. I thought maybe it was just good luck. Julián asked if I wanted breakfast and I said I didn't have anything in the house, so he said he would go out and get something while I got dressed. I'd slept in my clothes again, I was just so tired. Before I came here I was never tired – quite often I'd get in from parties at 3am, but I was never so tired that I even slept in my make-up, let alone fully dressed . And even when I was out late I rarely slept in until after 8. I'd have breakfast and then go to the gym for about 9 or 9.30, when most of the morning gym-goers had left for work, so I often had the place to myself. I was always full of energy. But here I felt different – almost ever since I arrived I felt like a zombie, like I'd had all the energy sapped out of me. Maybe I am a zombie, I'm not sure about anything anymore. I didn't even believe in zombies before, but now I think anything's possible. That's not true though, because I don't think it's possible that I'll get out of here. I just can't think properly anymore though, it would be easier if I could get all these cockroaches to be quiet so I could have some peace to try and make sense of it all, but they won't listen to me. They'll only listen to Julián. Nobody listens to me. I was trying to think about the breakfast wasn't I, so I could finish writing the story. Julián went out, and I got dressed. I didn't know what to wear – I wanted it to be something Julián would like. In the end I put on a yellow fifties-style sundress, the same one I'm wearing now. I'd had compliments before when I'd worn it, so I thought it was a good choice. I wonder if I would have still chosen it if I'd know it would be my last outfit. I actually couldn't even remember bringing it with me to Spain, but it was in the wardrobe so I must have done I guess. Or it got here somehow. I didn't really even question it at the time. I put my hair in a ponytail – I usually don't because I think it makes me look too much like a teenager, but I felt like it looked good with the dress and the sunshine. I made more of an effort with my make-up than I had done for a while – especially since I'd been here. I wanted Julián to think I looked pretty, so I put on some red lip gloss – red enough to be noticeable, but not too vampy for daytime – and eyeliner with a flick, which I thought would make me look young and flirty and carefree. I spritzed on the perfume I'd bought the day before, and hoped that Julián would be impressed. It was definitely an improvement on how he'd left me when he went out, so I thought that there was a good chance he would be. If he came back, anyway – I wasn't sure that he would after everything.

I walked around the house trying to tidy it up a bit while I had the chance, and I was in such a good mood that I even started singing that JLS song to myself - it's been in my head for some reason. I couldn't even remember the words properly so I was just humming some of them. If I die, would you come to my funeral? Would you cry? It was quite a gloomy song really, but I was in a good mood. I was tidying and singing and not even thinking about ghosts or anything else, and then I heard the door creak and I froze. But it was just Julián of course, letting himself back in. I was suddenly embarrassed in case he'd heard me singing, but if he had he didn't mention it. He'd brought some chocolate-covered pastries for breakfast that he said were called 'palmeritas', and some strawberries. He sat in his chair to eat, and I sat cross-legged on the bed. We hadn't eaten since lunchtime the day before, so I was really hungry again. Forgetting to eat wasn't something I could do before I came here, although I would have wished I could – I'd tried the fasting diet (I'd tried most diets at one time or another), and the fast days were complete torture to me. I generally ate quite healthily, and I was at the gym most days, but I still always wanted to lose weight. I think that's normal though when you're wearing a size ten, but you're at parties with models and actresses who could easily fit into an age ten. It's funny now though, because after all the time I spent worrying about it while I was alive, I'm probably thinner than any of them now. My arms are just bones. It's silly that I never noticed that the floorboards in this apartment are covered in bones. I couldn't see them before. There are just bones everywhere, and the cockroaches are climbing all over them. There are so many, I don't know where they all could have come from. Maybe they were all hiding behind the skirting board. Or maybe they were here the whole time like the bones, and I just didn't see them.

I wanted to ask Julián about his girlfriend, but I thought it was a bad time to bring it up while we were eating breakfast, especially since he hadn't really seemed like he wanted to talk about it when I asked him before. So instead I asked him about his family, and if they lived in Madrid too. He said he didn't have any family, and that he'd lived in lots of different cities but he'd been in Madrid for the last three years because of his work. I asked him how old he was and he wouldn't tell me, he just said that he was older than I probably thought he was. I didn't know what that meant, but I didn't want to ask again in case I annoyed him. He asked me what I'd been doing since I left university, and when I told him that I still hadn't had a job since graduating, he asked me what my dream job would be. I told him I would love to be a writer, and he told me that that was a good aspiration to have and that he would try to help me with it. Ben had never encouraged me to write, even though he knew that's what I really wanted to do. He said that if I tried to write a book it would be like saying that I was better than everyone else, and that the public would think I was a snob and hate me. He said that it was better for our image if I was a model or even a singer, which is how I ended up doing my underwear shoot. He never cared about what I wanted, just what was best for us. He just meant him of course. Now at last someone was really interested in me and cared about what I wanted. When Julián said that, I thought that everything that had happened had been worth it because it had brought me to this moment, because now I had someone who really cared about me and that meant that I was going to be happy. I couldn't imagine it working out any other way, but of course now I know that I couldn't have been any more wrong.

We finished our breakfast and Julián took the plates away and washed up. That was my last breakfast –

chocolate palmeritas and strawberries. My last meal in fact. If you're on death row you get to choose your last meal, but most of the time, the rest of us don't know at the time that we're eating our last meal. I certainly didn't. How far in advance do you have to choose your last meal when you're on death row, I wonder. What if you order a burger but then on the day you feel like roast pork? Can you change it? It must depend on what time of day you're having it too, because you couldn't really eat fish and chips or something like that until at least 12pm. I think that probably whatever you choose, when you're eating it you think about all the other things you could have chosen instead, and you regret the one you did choose. That must be awful, if you know you should have gone for the full English breakfast and now there's not going to be another chance. If you knew you were about to die, would you feel like eating anyway? Or would you just be too nervous and sick to eat? I wish I could eat. It's been a long time since that breakfast. It would just make me sick again though, and the stomach cramps are so bad, I feel like my stomach's being eaten away from the inside. Maybe that's what's happening. I can't ask anyone though, so I guess I'll never know. I don't know if it's really important to know exactly how I'm dying anyway. On the first day I felt like I was in worse pain than I had ever imagined in my life, but now I would be grateful to go back to that level of pain. The only thing that helps is passing out, which thankfully seems to be happening more often now, but still I keep coming back, and then I get that awful realisation of what's happening. Not for much longer though.

After breakfast, Julián asked me what I wanted to do that day. I said I hadn't really done much in Madrid except walk around the centre a bit, and he suggested that we could go to the botanic gardens. He said they were beautiful and one of his favourite places in Madrid. It sounded really nice – I love flowers, and I was also happy that Julián was suggesting spending the day together. I'd been half-expecting him not to come back after he went out to get breakfast, so this seemed almost like some kind of miracle. After everything I'd told him – not just about the ghosts but about Ben and everything else – I didn't feel like I'd really shown myself in the best light. But then I thought that maybe the fact that I instinctively opened up to him and told him things I wouldn't normally tell anyone, could perhaps be a sign that we had a deeper connection. And he definitely didn't seem scared off. I was amazed at how happy I felt in this house, when a couple of days before I couldn't imagine being here and feeling anything other than petrified, and like I was in terrible danger. Which is how I feel now of course. But at that time I felt completely safe with Julián around. It never occurred to me that the ghosts would come back. I thought that it was all over. I can't believe how naïve and stupid I was. How could I forget what I already knew, that

I would never be safe in this house? Nobody ever could be. But would I have preferred to know what was going to happen to me? If the outcome was inevitable then at least I had that short period of not being scared. But maybe it wasn't inevitable, maybe I didn't get drawn back here by some power beyond my control, and maybe I was the one in control and if I'd just trusted what I knew then I could have decided to go home, and I could have decided not to die. But was I ever in control? I thought I was at the time – it never occurred to me that I wouldn't be - but I just don't know now. Maybe everything that's ever happened to me was to lead me here. Maybe it wasn't really me who decided to move to Spain. Maybe everything was decided for me. Maybe I'm not to blame for it. That's what I'd prefer to believe.

I wonder how long it will take for someone to find me. It could be months – the rent's being paid by direct debit so nobody from the estate agency is going to come round to try and throw me out, and realistically my parents aren't even going to think anything of my lack of communication, at least until they get back from their cruise in a few weeks, and even if they start to worry they're not just going to immediately fly over here to check up on me. And when they do, what are they going to find? Not their daughter. More like something from a horror film. Or worse. I'm trying not to imagine what I'll look like as a corpse, especially once I've been decomposing for a while. They'll probably never get over it if they have to see me like that. Maybe they won't even be sure it's me and they'll have to wait for DNA results. And how will they even speak to the police anyway – they won't speak English. They'll need an interpreter to tell them it's their daughter's body. Maybe it will bring them closer together, but more likely they'll blame each other and never speak to each other again. Maybe they'll never speak again at all after that kind of trauma. I'm going to ruin their lives and I can't do anything to stop it. They might spend the rest of their lives trying to find out what happened to me, but they never will. They won't find this, and how could they ever know otherwise? There's no way they could ever guess what's happened, not in a million years. Nobody could. I'm not sure I even believe it myself still.

Julián was telling me about the botanic gardens, but I wasn't concentrating. He asked me if I was okay and I said I was, I was just tired still. He said maybe I was coming down with something and it might be better if we didn't go out. I really wanted to go out though, and I said maybe if I just had a rest for a while I'd be fine. I lay down on the bed and Julián sat in the armchair next to the bed, where he'd been all night. He asked if I wanted to sleep and I said no, I would just rest my eyes but I wanted him to keep talking to me. He asked what about and without even knowing I was going to do it, I said I wanted him to tell me about his girlfriend, the one who had died. He didn't say anything for a few seconds and I thought that I'd really done the wrong thing and made him angry with me. Maybe he would just get up and leave and I would never see him again. But he was still sitting in the chair, and finally he said that he hadn't been planning on doing this so soon, but perhaps it was the right time to tell me about her. He told me that her name was Elena and said that she was beautiful. His voice broke and I thought he might cry again. I found it really touching that he was so emotional, and it made him seem even more attractive. I'm ashamed to say I even felt a bit jealous of her. Does that mean I wished this on myself? I didn't mean that I wanted to be dead like her – it was just that he really seemed to love her and miss her, and I thought that if anything happened to me I would want there to be a handsome man to cry for me and light candles and tell people that I was beautiful. He didn't say anything for a while, and I thought he was trying not to cry. Then he cleared his throat and carried on telling me about her. He said that she was a nurse on the children's ward in the hospital, and that she loved her job and the children she looked after, and that she wanted to have children of her own too, but she never got the chance. Me neither. I would have liked a girl I think, but maybe that's because I never met a man I really wanted to have a child with, so whenever I thought about having children I could only ever imagine a child that looked just like I did in pictures from when I was a toddler. But I was starting to think I'd like to know what Julián looked like when he was a little boy. I wondered if he'd wanted to have children with Elena. I guessed that he had, because he'd brought up the subject and it was one of the only things he'd told me about her, but I didn't want to ask when he was clearly already upset. I asked how long it had been since she died, and he said it had only been a few months. That explained why he was still so emotional about it. I wondered if it had been a bad idea to bring him here and involve him in all the problems with the ghosts when the topic of death must still be really painful for him. I wondered how she had died, but I didn't want to upset him even more by making him tell me about what I thought must have been the most tragic event of his life. In my head I was imagining him having a knock on the door and answering it to two police officers who were telling him that his girlfriend had been knocked down by a car, and he was falling to the ground and sobbing. And then I was imagining that she was ill for a long time and at the end he was at her bedside holding her hand and stroking her forehead and talking to her, telling her she would be fine and shedding silent tears while she slipped away peacefully. I was half asleep and I couldn't really even tell if I was imagining these scenarios or if I was dreaming them or if they were really happening. I wanted to know what had really happened to Elena but I couldn't ask, and anyway I was too tired to speak, but I must have done because suddenly his voice started to break again and he said that she committed suicide – she killed herself with poison. I was falling asleep and I couldn't really process what he was saying. But I was thinking about poison when I fell to sleep and I had a really weird dream about Elena (because it was a dream I knew it was her even though I'd never seen her and in the dream she was a cartoon), and she was drinking different potions, like Alice in *Alice in Wonderland*, but instead of making her big and small, she was drinking them all and one of them made her neck grow really long like a giraffe, and then another one made her grow wings and she was flying all around and she was laughing, but then at the end she drank one and she and everything else went completely grey, as though the whole dream had turned into an old black-and-white film, and she started crying, and then she suddenly exploded and hundreds of cockroaches burst out and they all ran away in different directions. I felt the cockroaches running all over my body and I was jolted awake, screaming and trying to brush them off me. But there was nothing there, and Julián was stroking my forehead and telling me not to worry and that I'd just had a nightmare and there was nothing to be scared of. I didn't know how long I'd been asleep, or why I was still so tired. I said we should go because we still needed to get to the botanic gardens, but he said that I wasn't well and that it would be better to just stay here so I could rest. I started to feel a bit nervous about still being here when we'd only come to pick up the notebooks – I never meant to stay this long. And even though I felt safer with Julián here, I was still worried that if we didn't get out soon the ghosts might come back. And there was no way of telling how angry they would be if they did come back, or what they might do. But I didn't have the energy to try and persuade Julián that we should leave, and anyway I was so tired, and my eyes were trying to close again. I didn't want him to think I was rude though or that I didn't care about what he'd been telling me, and I apologised for falling asleep while he was talking. He said that it didn't matter and asked me what my nightmare had been about. I didn't want to tell him – I thought he might think that I was making light of his pain and Elena's death – so I just made up a story about dreaming that I was at a wild animal park and being chased around by a giant emu that was trying to peck me. That was actually a true story from when I was little, but I can't say I've ever had nightmares about it. He seemed to believe it though. Then an emu was here in the apartment, but it wasn't trying to peck me and actually it said that it could fly me home, but I can't remember why I didn't go. But maybe I was just writing about it and I got confused and thought it was here. I'm sure I remember it being here though. Why didn't I just go home with it if it was here? I don't know, but it doesn't matter now anyway. I just need to keep writing and then go, and stop thinking that I can change things. I can't change it. But I'm so scared. I want the pain to end, but

I'm so terrified of what comes afterwards. I need to stop getting so confused though, because otherwise even if someone ever reads it they won't be able to understand anything, and I want them to know what happened to me.

When I told Julián the made-up nightmare story about the emu, he said that it was normal to have nightmares after what I'd been through, and that he had had nightmares too after Elena died. He said that he sometimes dreamed that she had survived and they were still together, and that they went for walks and normal things, and then he'd wake up and remember that she was gone and it was even worse than the first time. Then he said that other times he had weird nightmares about her being a cartoon character and drinking cartoon poison and exploding. It was really strange, because he was describing the exact dream I had just had, but how could he have known what I was dreaming? I don't think I told him, I'm sure I told him the emu one instead, but it's so hard to remember now. I thought that maybe the apartment had put the nightmare into my head somehow. I never had nightmares normally, but this place was just full of darkness and fear and sadness. Or maybe it just showed that we had some kind of subconscious connection. I didn't want to tell him I'd had the same dream, and I thought that if I told him the truth now he'd know that I'd lied to him, or he might think I was pretending to make fun of him, so I just kept quiet. I changed the subject and said we should go out and do something and not just waste the day, especially in this apartment where things could start happening again at any moment. He said that tomorrow we would go out and do fun things and that then I would start to feel more normal, but for now it was better for me to just get some rest and not try to do too much. He mentioned the botanic gardens again, and then he said that the Prado was a really interesting place to visit too, and suggested that we could go there in the afternoon after we'd been to the gardens. I told him that everyone in London had recommended it too and it was the first place I'd visited when I got here, but it was so huge that I'd only seen parts of it. He asked me if I'd seen Goya's *Black Paintings* and I said that I had and that they were my favourites in the Prado even though I found them very unsettling. I realised that after being so impressed by them when I saw them, I actually hadn't thought about them again since, but then I'd been so preoccupied by what was happening here that I hadn't really had the chance to think about anything else. I wanted to lighten the mood a bit, mainly because I'd started to feel a bit scared and on edge again, and I made a joke that if Goya's paintings were a reflection of what was going on in his mind, he must have had some quite strange nightmares too. Julián told me that when Goya was an old man, he was living alone and had various health problems and was also traumatised from years spent going into war zones to paint what was happening, and that he had basically been driven mad. He said that Goya used to paint these grotesque images directly onto the walls of his living room and other rooms in the house, and he was a recluse and had no visitors so nobody even saw them until after he died. He just lived alone with all of that darkness everywhere he went in the house. It must have been like living in Hell, and he had created it himself. I thought that it was so strange, and I couldn't imagine why he would possibly want to do that, but then it occurred to me that isn't that what I've done too? Created my own Hell? I definitely haven't done it deliberately, but I can't help thinking that I have nobody else to blame but myself. Anyway, I don't know why I keep dwelling on blame when there's nothing I can do now. I told Julián that I would like to go back to the Prado and see those paintings again, especially as he seemed to know some of the background to them. I really did want to go back, I just couldn't understand why I was so exhausted. I was thirsty, but I was too tired to get up, and before I even had enough energy to ask Julián to get me a drink I had already fallen asleep again. I thought I had just closed my eyes for a second, but when I opened them again Julián was still sitting there but he had got a glass of water from somewhere. Maybe I had said something after all, or he just knew somehow what I was thinking about. It was dark, and I realised I must have been asleep for quite a long time, although I had been feeling so drowsy and confused all day that I wasn't sure of what time of day it had been when I fell asleep. I wondered what the time was. I could hear a clock ticking loudly, and I thought it was strange because I hadn't seen one in the apartment. I realised that it had been ticking the whole time I'd been in this apartment, but I hadn't paid attention enough to question it before. It was only when I woke up and wanted to know the time that I even thought about a clock and realised there wasn't one. I asked Julián what time it was and he just said that it was late and we would have to sleep here again. I told him we couldn't because things had happened here before and just because it had been okay so far, there was no way of knowing what might happen if we stayed and I didn't want us to push our luck. He just told me what he'd told me before, that the ghosts wouldn't come back while he was here and I should trust him. I started to feel frustrated because I wanted him to understand what had happened to me and I felt like he wasn't taking it seriously enough. I knew I needed to get out of here but I felt too weak to explain it to him. I was nearly crying and I told him he didn't understand and that we needed to leave, even if he had to carry me out of here, and for the first time since I'd met him he looked angry. He told me that I was the one who didn't understand, and that he knew better than anyone about the ghosts in this house. I was angry too. I told him that that didn't make any sense – nobody could ever understand what I'd been going through in this place. He told me he understood perfectly, because this was Elena's apartment and she went through exactly the same thing.

Suddenly nothing made any sense anymore. Elena had lived here? A million questions came into my head but I couldn't get any of them out. Finally I asked him if that was why she killed herself. He spoke in a quiet voice and told me it was. He said that she'd lived there for a couple of months before she died, and the haunting had started as soon as she moved in, but she was too nervous to tell him about it in case he thought she was crazy and left her. But she'd been petrified – every night she'd heard the sobbing and screaming and she'd even seen the ghosts, not just their shadows. She was too afraid to sleep, and she was exhausted to the point of fainting at work on more than one occasion and even once in the street, but she'd kept that a secret from him too. Julián said she seemed so distant and withdrawn, and nothing he did seemed to make her happy anymore, and he had started to suspect that she was having an affair. But when he confronted her, she burst into tears and told him about everything that was happening and how it was ruining her life, and he'd believed her and come here to stay with her and to try to protect her. As soon as he arrived it all stopped, and after a while they both thought the ghosts had gone and they were safe. He said that his biggest regret was that he actually started to think that maybe she had just imagined it. Anyway, he thought that whatever had been happening had stopped, and it wouldn't happen again. That's why, when he had to go away on a work trip for a few days he thought it was safe to leave her here alone while he was away. They were both convinced that the haunting was over and the ghosts were gone forever. She told him she'd be fine, and that she wasn't afraid anymore. But while she was there on her own they came back, even worse than before. They must had been angry that she had brought him here to protect her, and they took their revenge while she was alone and vulnerable. She hadn't been able to explain to him exactly what had happened, but whatever it was, it had driven her completely out of her mind and she poisoned herself. When he got back from his business trip, she was still alive but it was too late to save her, and he waited with her to take care of her until the end. So she died in this house, I asked him. He said yes, that she had died here in bed. The bed I was lying in. As soon as I heard that it started to feel different – I could almost smell death around me, and I knew I shouldn't be here. I asked him why he didn't take her to hospital. He said it was already too late when he got to her, and she didn't want to die in hospital with so much noise and doctors and nurses rushing around everywhere, and she especially didn't want to see the looks on the faces of her colleagues when they saw her. She just wanted him to stay with her, and she was in so much pain that she couldn't stand to be moved anyway. She was constantly crying and moaning, begging him to just kill her to stop the pain. Later she started hallucinating and would talk to people who weren't there and talk to him about things that weren't happening, and he just went along with it because he didn't want to cause her any more distress. He told me the days he spent with her before her death were the worst of his life. In the end she didn't have the energy to talk or even cry, and then all he could do was hold her hand, a hand that didn't look or feel like Elena's hand anymore, until eventually she slipped away. He told me that the experience had traumatised him so much that he hadn't been able to go to work or even leave his house for weeks. He felt like he had failed her, because if he'd just stayed with her like he had promised to then she would have been fine and nothing bad would have happened to her. He said that I was the first woman he'd spoken to since Elena's death – he wasn't interested in meeting anyone new yet, but something had drawn him to me in the cathedral. Then when we were having lunch and I told him about the ghosts, he instantly knew that I must live in the same apartment, and he felt like he was being given a second chance to make things right by saving me. It was all too much for me to take in. Why would he risk coming back here after what had happened? He didn't even know me – why would he put himself through this to try and save me? But I felt comforted to know that someone really understood this. I was convinced that as long as he stayed here, I would be okay. But I knew that to be truly safe I still needed to get out of here, and I couldn't do that until I managed to get some rest so I could have the energy to get out. With all the thoughts in my head after what Julián had just told me, I doubted that I would manage to fall asleep again, but of course I did.

Day 6

I woke up a lot during the night. Even when I was asleep I couldn't settle, I was scared the ghosts would come back. We'd stayed too long. I had nightmares I think – they were the kind that you can't remember anything about when you wake up, but you still know that you've been having nightmares and feel weirdly panicked and uneasy. But every time I jumped awake and opened my eyes I could see that Julián was still there, sitting in his usual chair and watching over me, and I felt better. I'd never seen him sleep, and every time I woke up I thought how tired he must be, but I didn't say anything about it, I just smiled and he smiled back and then I closed my eyes again.

I don't know when it was morning. It never gets light in here now so it's hard to tell. At some point I woke up and didn't fall back to sleep again immediately, and I propped myself up in bed and we started talking. He did anyway – I still wasn't really with it so I just listened to him, although I couldn't really concentrate. We didn't have breakfast this time. I didn't even think about it, I felt so exhausted even after sleeping for however long it was that it didn't occur to me to be hungry. He was still smiling – I didn't understand how he could still be smiling when he didn't seem to have slept at all for the last two nights. He was talking about something and I was trying to listen, but I could feel myself falling back to sleep until the name

Elena caught my attention. He was talking about her again. He was saying that Elena used to keep a diary, and after she died he liked to read it and that that was the only way that he could feel closer to her and it helped him remember her.

He asked me if I kept a diary. I said no, mainly because I was too tired to speak much, but also because the only time I ever kept a diary was when I was in year eight, and it was more of a weekly update on who I was in love with. I wonder where they all are now. I never kept in touch with many people from school, but I do hear about some of them sometimes, mainly from my mum because she socialises with their parents. Some of them are bankers and lawyers, and quite a few of them are like me and don't work at all, or they started their own businesses that never made any money so they still live off their parents but call themselves entrepreneurs. A few went into music and acting, also funded by their parents. And then a couple of the more obnoxious ones went into *Made in Chelsea.* I wish I could change lives with any of them now though. I try to imagine myself being somewhere else and having a different life, doing anything other than this. Sometimes I imagine I'm going for a walk in the countryside with a big dog and then coming home and painting. Things I never even did when I was alive, and probably never would have done. But it's funny that even with all the pain, it's surprisingly easy to make yourself believe you're somewhere else and that none of it is happening. Not for long though. You always remember again, and then maybe it's even worse than the first time. It's like when you get your heart broken and you cry yourself to sleep, and then in the morning you wake up and for a few seconds you just feel a bit dozy in a nice way, and then you remember everything and your heart sinks. It's like that, except a million times worse.

He told me I should start keeping a journal. He said that when you write down your thoughts it helps you understand what you're really thinking and everything seems clearer. And he also said that it's important to do it because otherwise after you die you're gone forever, but if you have a journal it's as though you're still alive in some way when people read what you've written. He asked me if I would like to read Elena's journal. I said that it felt wrong, like I would be invading her privacy, but he said no, it wasn't meant to be private and it might help me. I wondered what she had written about. Probably the ghosts. Maybe she wrote about what happened when he was away and why she felt like she had no option but to kill herself. Or maybe she wrote it before, and she stopped when bad things started to happen because she didn't want to think about what was going on, and writing about it would make it real. Or maybe she was too embarrassed to write about it in case someone read it and thought she was crazy.

I told him that maybe next time we saw each other I could read it, once we were out of here. But he told me he already had it with him, and he wanted me to read it now. I felt sorry for him. I thought he must keep her journal in his bag to feel closer to her. I still didn't feel like it was the right time to read it, especially if it was going to be about the ghosts – what if talking about them made them come back? It wasn't safe. I didn't want to hurt his feelings though, so I said okay, but maybe he could read some of it to me because I was too tired to read. Then I realised that obviously it would be in Spanish so I wouldn't be able to understand any of it anyway. But he said he could translate it for me. He said he'd read it so many times he'd practically memorised it, and it wouldn't be difficult for him to tell me what it meant in English. I still wasn't sure it was the right thing to do, but in a way I was curious, and anyway he was so insistent that I was worried he'd get angry again if I argued about it, so I didn't try to stop him.

But instead of getting it out of his bag, he went over to the shelf and picked up one of the notebooks that I'd found hidden in the wall, the one on the top of the pile, and came and sat back down in his chair. I was confused, I told him that it was one of the notebooks I'd found earlier in the week, not Elena's dairy. He just said that this was

Elena's diary. But it couldn't be, because he'd just said that he read Elena's diary all the time, and I knew for a fact that this one had been hidden in my wall and he'd only seen it for the first time last night. So how could it be hers? I didn't really know what to say, but I said that it didn't make sense that it could be hers. He just smiled. He asked if I wanted to know what it said. I said I was more interested in what it was doing hidden behind my wall. He sighed, and said that when he got back from his business trip and found her dying, she told him that after she poisoned herself she had started writing a journal about what it was like to die, and everything that had happened here that had led her to kill herself. After she died he had read it over and over again. He didn't want to because it was so painful for him, but he knew that if he kept it in his house he wouldn't be able to stop himself. He couldn't throw it away or destroy it because it was hers, and it would be disrespectful to her memory to do that, so he hid it here in her apartment expecting nobody to ever find it. That's why when I mentioned finding the notebooks, he knew I'd found Elena's diary and he had to come back here to make sure that I didn't throw it out, and because he felt like he needed to read it again.

I felt bad for not trusting him. But I wondered about the others. Were they all Elena's? It didn't make sense. They were all written in different handwriting, so how could they be? I asked him what the other notebooks were, and why he'd hidden them with Elena's. He didn't say anything for a few seconds, then he answered and confused me even more. Elena wasn't the first person to die in this house, he told me. Now I really didn't know what to say. How could this make sense? I asked him how he knew. He told me he was bored of all these questions and I obviously didn't trust him so maybe he should just leave. I don't know why, but for some reason I apologised and asked him to stay. I said I was just tired and I felt like I was coming down with something, and maybe that was why none of it was making sense to me. He said it was okay. Then he told me that they all start acting like this in the end, asking too many questions. I asked him what he meant, and who he was talking about, and he just stared at me coldly and said he was bored of all my stupid questions, and that I was stupid and that's why I deserved what was going to happen to me. He laughed and said that if I wasn't so stupid I might have bothered to learn some Spanish before I came, and then I would have understood what they'd written on the wall and got out, like they'd told me to. Lucky for him I was so stupid, he told me. Unlucky for me.

Then he held out the glass of water for me to drink. I knew it would kill me. I didn't want to drink it. I didn't want to die, and more than that I didn't want to do it to myself. I didn't want to just obey him – I wanted to refuse and say no and stand up to him. But somehow I saw my hand reach out and take it. I tried to just drop the glass on the floor, but I couldn't. My hand wasn't under my control anymore. Nothing was. I had to obey him, like all of the others did. My hand put the glass to my mouth and I took a sip. It tasted vile. I wanted to spit it out but of course I couldn't. He was watching me and smiling. I wanted to throw the glass in his face and make him stop smiling, but there was no way I could do that. I just carried on drinking until the glass was empty, then my hand dropped the glass and it rolled off the bed onto the floor. There was nothing I could do now.

He told me it was time to start writing. I don't know where he got this new notebook from – all the ones in the pile I'd found had been written in already. He handed it to me with the pen. I said I didn't have anything to write and I wasn't going to do anything he said but he said that of course I would do it and it was better for me not to make a fuss and upset myself, because in the end he would win and nothing I did would change that. I didn't pick up the pen though. For hours I just sat there. I was in so much pain. I couldn't get up. I begged him to call an ambulance and he laughed at me. He asked me what I thought an ambulance was going to do. He told me that the sooner I started writing, the sooner all of this would be over. He said that I just had to write about what had happened in this house, and when I finished writing the pain would end. I didn't want to die though, I wanted to survive, but after a few days or maybe hours I couldn't stand the pain, and apart from that I thought at least it might distract me a bit, because lying in a bed in so much pain and vomiting everywhere while the person who did it to you just stares at you with such a horrible smile on their face is worse than I could ever imagine Hell being. So I started writing. I wrote about coming here and being so excited when I first arrived, and about the crying in the night and the wonderful hotel and the cockroaches and the notebooks and meeting Julián and about what he did to me. And that's it. I've said everything I needed to say. Another notebook for the next girl to find.

He was always watching me. He didn't look like Julián anymore, although I suppose anyone else looking at him would say he looked exactly the same as he always had. But when I looked at him I knew now why I felt like I recognised him when I first met him. He reminded me of the Goya painting. He was the He-Goat. Of course he was. He's still smiling, but his eyes are so cold and full of evil. When I first saw him I noticed something about his eyes, but I didn't know what it was. Now I know, but now it's too late. He was right – I was stupid. I don't know how I didn't see all of this from the start. None of the others saw it though either. I wondered how many there were. How many of these death diaries had I found? Eight, was it? So there were at least that many girls. I asked him how many others there were before me and he didn't answer.

I told him he'd got me now so he had nothing to lose by telling me the truth, but he still ignored me. I asked if it was eight, and then he laughed and said that I had underestimated him. So there must be more, but how many I don't know. He wouldn't tell me anything. He just told me to get on with writing my own story and I would meet the others soon anyway. I don't want to die, but in a way it will be easier I think. At least I'll be free from him, until he brings the next one here. I wish I'd understood that they were trying to warn me about him. I thought I was being strong by staying and trying not to be scared, or at least trying to act as though I wasn't scared, but they just wanted me to leave here and be safe. I thought when he came here they stopped because he was protecting me, but they were just too afraid of him to stay. Either that or he forced them to leave somehow because he didn't want them trying to save me. I wonder if they ever do manage to save anyone. I doubt it though - he's more powerful than they are.

The cockroaches are everywhere now. Everything is silence except for the scuttling of the cockroaches and the ticking of the clock that isn't there. It's funny, because I used to be scared of the cockroaches, I didn't want them to touch me. But now they crawl all over me and I don't even flinch anymore or try to brush them off me. When I was at university I read a story by a woman, maybe Portuguese or Brazilian, Clara or Clarice something. I can't really think anymore, but it was something about a cockroach, and the woman in the story kills the cockroach and then she eats it, because she feels like she has a relationship with the cockroach or it's like her in some way or something. I don't feel anything for these cockroaches, but I don't hate them now. I don't think I could eat one either though, even though I'm so hungry. I don't think I could physically eat anymore. I've already vomited everything out. It's everywhere. It's not food anymore. For a while it was just blood, bright red, and now it's black. I don't know what that means. Maybe it's my intestines being dissolved. Can that happen? What does it matter now anyway? I'm dying, that's all I know and maybe that's all I need to know. Surely it can't take much longer. The room's filling up with water. I don't know where it's coming from. Someone once told me that drowning was a nice way to die, but I didn't believe it. I still don't.

He never speaks to me. He just watches. Once I've finished writing this, all that's left to do is wait. I don't think I'll have long to wait. I hope not. The last thing I'll see is his face and that sneering smile. I don't want to die like this but I can't move. I can't do anything. I'll always be here now, none of us can ever leave. I don't know who's crying now. Are the others here? Maybe it's just me. Maybe I was the one crying all along. The water is still rising. Soon it will be over my head. I can still hear the clock ticking, but not for long. Nobody can help me, it's too late. The Great He-Goat is still just sitting and watching me, and smiling.

Printed in Great Britain
by Amazon.co.uk, Ltd.,
Marston Gate.

9607276R00074